Murderous Karma

The Veils of Parallel Times Trilogy
— Book 3 —

C.J. Carson

RUSTIC BARN
Publishing

Published by:
Rustic Barn Door Publishing
www.cjcarsonauthor.com
cjcarsonauthor@gmail.com

ISBN: 978-1-954356-02-3

Library of Congress Control Number:

Interior Design by TWA Solutions

For DMD, who for the last forty years has encouraged me to keep moving towards every dream I have chased, joined me on every adventure I have traveled and held me up whenever the road of life got rough.

Acknowledgments

I humbly thank my friends and family who continue to support my efforts in challenging my imagination, writing stories, and creating characters they grow to love.

My daughter continues on this journey with me. She is my loyal beta reader who reads everything I send her. She is part of the magic that helps me create a world where my characters thrive and grow against all odds. For that, I say, with all my heart and love, thank you!

Sincere gratitude to my fantastic editor, Jessica Tilles, who works diligently to keep me focused. She was vital in helping me bring all the books in this trilogy to life on the pages.

This writing journey has been beyond anything I had expected. The wonderful emails, Facebook and Twitter posts about my books from readers who love the characters, and the wonderful people I've met at various events, has been a heart-warming and humbling experience. I have enormous gratitude for everyone who have become fans of Allie and Claudia. I am deeply grateful for your support. I sincerely thank you for reading my books. Hang on tight, this ride isn't ending any time soon.

Prologue

For those who don't know me, my name is Allie Callahan, and today, I am a different person than I was a year and a half ago. My life experiences have imparted a pearl of wisdom upon me, teaching me that life's circumstances can change us in profound ways, shaping who we become and how we choose to live. If we listen to our inner voices, we can grow, shedding the cocoon or those parts of ourselves that no longer serve us, allowing us to blossom into a miraculous butterfly, soaring off toward our destined paths.

In my not-so-distant past, I was an overachiever and successful businesswoman. In fact, a journalist from a local paper once described me as "a highly driven, high-powered executive who ran her family's marketing firm with her brother, Mark Callahan." The reality is not so simple. Beyond the veil of my success, the journalist didn't see that my business consumed me. Having a moment for anything more was non-existent. I had no space for a relationship of any kind, no room for a personal or social life. I was too wrapped up in my work to notice I was missing one. It is a blessing that life's circumstances has, once again, carried me this far. Now I can muster the faith and courage to accept and embrace my gifts that I continue to discover.

My hesitancy in the past grew from the loss of my only links I had left to my Native American history: the passings of my father and grandfather. For years, I have suppressed my bestowed gifts, burying them and quashing them from my memories. Rediscovering and embracing my gifts from the universe will allow me to use them for the good of others. However, before that can happen, I must conquer my nemesis, Makya, who possess the same gifts. Unfortunately, his greed continues to lead him down a path that feeds his insatiable lust for power and dominance. He has to be stopped. Possessing such powerful gifts brings about responsibilities and challenges. Makya's demise is my responsibility and challenge, one I must face alone. For only I can put an end to his reign.

Now, my journey brings me to the edge of a precipice in my natural life, and, I guess, that is where this part of my story begins.

Chapter 1

It had been a long and trying day. I was looking forward to dinner with my mother and Guile, who had moved into the penthouse apartment at the Summit. That evening, they invited me, Josh, my fiancé, Claudia, my best friend, and her new husband, Jake, to dinner. Guile prepared the most amazing prime rib. It was so tender it nearly melted in our mouths. He served it with roasted potatoes and asparagus spears. Except for a few delicate blindsiding moments, when I tried to evade certain topics of conversation, it went off without a hitch.

Since Josh and I had been missing in action for several months, we no longer had an apartment or a place to stay. Claudia and Jake were gracious to invite us to stay with them in their apartment on the eleventh floor of the Summit until we could sort things out and get our own place. After dinner that evening, when we returned to Claudia and Jake's apartment, we were more than ready to turn in. Within a few minutes, I turned to Josh, wrapped my arms around him, and planted a gentle kiss on his lips. Sliding my hands down his neck, I grabbed his collar, pulling him toward the bedroom, calling out, "Goodnight, you guys. Josh and I are going to bed. See you in the morning!"

Brick, our Doberman Pinscher, and the newest member of our family, followed Josh and me into the bedroom, went to his big cushy bed, and lay down. Kneeling, I ran my hand over his sleek black coat and hugged his neck. "You are such a good boy, Brick. We are so lucky to have you in our lives. We're going to give you the forever home you deserve. Right, Josh?"

Looking across the room, Josh was slithering into bed, pulling the covers up over his head. His muffled voice, wrapped in a moan, came through the bedding. "I think maybe I had just one glass of wine too many. I can't seem to keep my eyes open."

Moving over to him, I pulled the comforter back from his face and planted a kiss on his cheek. "That's okay, honey. I think I will take a quick shower and join you."

By the time I showered and returned, Josh was sound asleep. Climbing into bed next to him, I lay there in the dark, wide awake, as I recounted the day's events through my head. Even dinner had its challenging moments. The incident I had with a glass of wine and the sensation I got as I swirled the sweet spirit in the glass. It was the first time I felt myself slipping from my body. If I hadn't lost my grip, shattering the glass on the floor, I think I would have slipped away again, right there in front of everyone.

I lifted the gold chain that hung around my neck, holding the tree of life pendant passed down to me by my ancestors, and the key I had snuck out of the evidence room in the morgue that afternoon. Not my finest moment. Then, it came to me. *That's it. I think I can will myself to travel back to the hunting lodge on purpose.* Focusing on the necklace, I spun it in a circle. Dazed, I concentrated on the memory of my travel to the hunting lodge, where I married James, that version of Josh from that time.

With great suddenness, I found myself thrust back in time to the 1920s. Instead of the lodge, I was in that beautiful Ford Model T. I was there again, not as Allie, but Anna. I was waiting with Jeremy while James climbed the stairs and disappeared into that small wooden chapel. Jeremy opened my door to help me out of the car. As he took my hand, I gazed into his eyes. He was my dear friend, Dakota, from my current life, not Jeremy. With a slight hesitation and a tilt of his head, he helped me from the car.. "Are you ready, Anna?"

"I am."

Helping me out of the car, he led me up the stairs and into the entryway to the chapel. As the church organ began playing, Jeremy escorted me from the back of the sanctuary and up the aisle to James, who was standing on the altar, beaming from ear to ear.

The ceremony was brief and beautiful.

The pastor announced, "James, you may now kiss your bride."

As James kissed me, that strong and familiar connection I knew so well consumed me.

Interrupting, the pastor chuckled. "Okay, James, come up for some air. It's time to walk your new bride to the hall in the next room for a small celebration with your family."

Several people had gathered around a piano playing ragtime music as we entered the small reception area. The tune sounded familiar, but I couldn't quite place it.

As James and I moved across the room, the group parted, exposing an old player piano. On the floor next to it was that familiar brown leather satchel.

The gentleman on the piano stool spun around to face us, and as he reached up for something at his neck, a look of panic washed over his face. Staring into his eyes, it was Makya looking back at me. I could tell by his expression that he recognized me, not as the bride, but as his nemesis.

Lifting the chain to pull the key and pendant out from the front of my dress, I called out, "Is this what you're looking for?"

His expression spoke volumes. He knew it was over.

Opening my pearl clutch, I pulled out a small .38-caliber pistol. Clutching it with both hands, I aimed and pulled the trigger.

Chapter 2

Much like awakening from a horrible nightmare, I jolted into my body with my heart pounding. I rolled over to Josh, laying on the other side of our California king-sized bed. The clock on the dresser read 3:00 a.m.

Laying in the darkness, a sense of relief overcame me. There was still work to be done, but I had finally penetrated the bubble that surrounded my archenemy, Makya. The armored wall that insulated him from my attempts to stop him had come tumbling down.

I knew I wouldn't be able to fall back to sleep. I needed to get in touch with Brian, our forensic specialist, and get him to open the morgue for me. Picking up my cell phone from the nightstand, I slipped into the bathroom to call Detective Payne Brian from forensics.

Answering on the fourth ring, he cleared his throat and forced out, "Hello, Payne here!"

Trying not to wake Josh, I whispered as quietly as I could. "Payne, it's Allie. Do you think you and Brian could meet me at the morgue?"

"Now?"

"Yes, now."

"Why?"

"I think I'm on the verge of making a breakthrough in my case, but I need to get to the morgue to know for sure."

"Allie, it's three o'clock in the morning!"

"I know Payne, I'm sorry, but I can't sleep. Please! If I'm right, you won't be sorry, I promise!"

"Okay, but stay there. I'll pick up Brian, and we'll come to you. We'll be there inside of forty-five minutes."

As I hung up, I debated whether I should wake Josh from his sound sleep. He would be furious if he woke, and I had left without telling him. Giving him a gentle nudge, I whispered, "Hey, Josh, wake up."

Rolling over, he reached across the bed to me. "What? Allie, what time is it?"

Placing my fingers over his lips, I shushed him. "You'll wake Claudia and Jake. It's three-fifteen, and Payne is coming over to pick me up. We're going to the morgue."

Shocked, he leaned up on his elbow. "What? Why? Can't you sleep a few more hours and go in at seven?"

"No, Josh, I have to check on something. You stay here, and I'll see you when you get to the station in a few hours."

"No way. I'm coming."

"No, Josh, get some sleep. I'll be with Payne and Brian, and if it makes you feel better, I'll take the dog."

After promising to take Brick with me, he conceded.

Moving in his direction, I leaned in to kiss him on the cheek. "I love you, Josh. I'll see you in a few hours."

Getting up, I got dressed, made a coffee to go, and made my way to the foyer with Brick in record time.

Officer Antonio Moretti, assigned as our security, was sitting in the foyer in a high-back chair. As I attempted to explain, there was a knock at the door.

He stood. "This must be Payne. He called and said he was on his way over."

"Yes, and he got here quicker than I thought he would."

Chapter 3

Payne, Brian, and I left the Summit and were at the station by four-fifteen. We headed down to the morgue, and as we entered, Brian turned on the overhead light.

Gazing at the three metal tables covered with sheets, I stepped over to the table closest to us. I pulled the sheet back, exposing several items we had disassembled from the cube the day before.

Moving to the second table, I pulled back that sheet to a body splayed out like a jigsaw puzzle.

Looking perplexed, Payne stepped in front of me. "Allie, what are you looking for?"

Approaching the last table, I held my breath and snatched off the third sheet. Spinning, I faced Brian and Payne. "That! That's what I was looking for!"

Laying on the table was more debris from the cube, which included pieces of a brown leather satchel, unspent ammunition, a couple of automatic weapons, and a .38-caliber gun.

Brian was even more confused as he moved over to the table and rifled through the items. "Allie, what do you see? I don't get it."

I stepped directly in front of him. "There's only one body."

"Well, yes, but—"

"Look, guys. I think we need to go out to Brian's office to have this conversation. Let's go sit down, have a coffee, and talk about this. I think I have some explaining to do."

Moving to the office, we grabbed a coffee and sat down at the small, round conference table.

Leaning back in his chair, Brian stretched his arms out over his head and then back down, grabbing his chin and cracking his neck. "Allie, could you please tell me why you dragged us out of a sound sleep this morning just to get here and look over the evidence we uncovered yesterday? Why couldn't this wait for a few more hours?"

"God, Brian, I hate when you adjust your own neck like that. It's so bad for you." Standing, I began pacing the floor with Brick at my heels, who seemed to sense my concern. Pointing to his bed that Payne had purchased for him, I said, "Go lie down, boy."

"It's not bad for me. No one knows the vertebra in my spine any better than I do. I can adjust my own back. Come on, for crying out loud, you need to get to the point. Why are we here at the crack of dawn this morning?"

Trying to make a joke, I spun away from them, chuckled, and in my best Scottish accent blew out, "A bit cranky this morning, aren't we?"

The room was silent for a few seconds. Then Brian burst out laughing.

Spinning again to face them, I thought, *Here goes.* "Look, as strange as this may sound, many important articles are missing from these tables."

Payne stretched his neck from side to side, turning to Brian. "What is she talking about? What did you find yesterday that has gone missing over the past several hours?" Wide-eyed, they both turned to me as Payne gasped. "Unless..."

Before Brian could respond, with a sheepish grin, I pleaded, "Well, for starters, the pieces of navy-blue fabric from a pinstriped suit, as well as some white wool fabric from a man's fedora hat." I walked over and peered through the observation window to the morgue. "And the most crucial thing that is missing is a second body! A second body is missing! Yesterday, when we untangled that cube of objects, we found two bodies. One was a woman, and the other clearly had the stature of a man."

Brian stood, joining me at the window. "Allie, what are you talking about? All we found in that twisted mess of debris was what you see there on the tables right now. Nothing is missing. Are you saying that you believe I could forget an entire second body in the span of twelve hours? Even if that was remotely true, where could it have gone?"

Turning, I leaned against the wall and then pushed off of it, projecting myself across the room. "That's not exactly what I'm saying."

Brian shook his head, letting out an audible breath. "Alrighty then, I can't wait to hear this one."

Payne walked over to the coffeemaker. "Anyone care to join me for another shot of caffeine?"

I rolled my shoulders and neck as we sat down, trying to wake my body up a bit more. I took a sip of coffee and wiped a drip that landed on my lip with a napkin. Damn, it was hot. Placing my cup on the table, I pursed my lips and rolled my eyes.

"You know that I have done some traveling in my recent history. Some rather involuntary traveling to other times in the past or different dimensions. I haven't quite sorted that all out yet, but you know what I mean. Right? To just some other level of consciousness? Well, so to speak.

"Payne, do you remember the day I met Dakota's father, Paco? It was at the beginning of this entire investigation. In fact, it was the very same day I met that young Native American girl named Tanis."

"How could I forget! You passed out cold the minute you laid eyes on her!"

"That's right, but more importantly, do you remember why I passed out? It was from the shock of seeing her. Don't you remember my telling you that there was a picture of Tanis on the wall the previous day among those with Makya's victims? That picture was missing, and no one remembered ever seeing it but me. When she walked in that day, I was so shocked, I passed out because I recognized her as a girl I saved in my dream the night before. I remembered it all so clearly. When we asked her what she remembered, she said it was difficult to talk about, but that for her, it happened seven years before. She told us it occurred in front of the Rockland Hotel, which was sold and is now the Summit. She was so clear about the date because it happened on her birthday. Her friends had thrown her a birthday party, and she was walking home when it happened.

"Look, the point is, seven years before, a woman came out of the Summit, or I guess for her the Rockland Hotel, saved her, and then disappeared. In my reality, I saved her the night before in a dream and then immediately woke from that dream. Well, I thought it was a dream. You and I both know that was more than just a dream! Back then, I was just beginning to understand all of this, but now..."

I paused for their response, but they just stood there as if they were waiting for the next proverbial shoe to drop.

"Well, last night, I discovered a way to do that of my own free will. Well, what I mean is that I found a way to travel back in time on my own. I was able to control it. Well, kind of."

Payne shook his head. "Okay, wait a minute, Allie! What does 'kind of' mean? You could kind of move through time?"

Knowing how crazy I sounded, I thought for a second. I fingered the necklace around my neck. "This pendant is the tree of life. I was told that if I wear it, I will stay grounded, but I have learned that it will always bring me home where I belong, to my true time. It will also permit me to go into a state or a level of consciousness that will allow me to travel willingly to other lives."

Brian looked even more puzzled than he did before. Plopping down in his chair at the table, he nodded. "Well, what does this have to do with what we found in the cube yesterday?"

Carefully collecting my thoughts, I looked at them. "I think I may have altered history a little last night."

Brian sprung from his chair. "What? Do you know how devastating the consequences of that could be?"

"Wait, hear me out. I know what you're saying, but I think I need to go back and undo or change only those things that Makya has already altered or changed in the past. You should have seen his face when he recognized me during that time period. I believe it is my job to stop him once and for all, but it has to be back in whatever time he started changing the past. I have to figure that out and go there to stop him once and for all.

"When I traveled back in time, I went with a little more knowledge than I had the last time I was there. Last night when I traveled, I went back with that knowledge, and I was able to change everything. I know you don't remember because, for you, it never happened. What you are missing is that yesterday, when we took that cube apart, there were two bodies. One was a version of me and the other a version of Josh from the 1920s. Last night, when I traveled back to the twenties, I killed that version of Makya from that lifetime. So now the body laying in there on the table is him. When we finish going through the rest of the evidence, I believe we will find that the man on the table was shot to death by a .38-caliber pistol. I know this because I am the one who shot him."

Neither Brian nor Payne spoke.

"Don't either of you have something to say?"

Payne shook his head. "I'm not sure what to say. Wait, does that mean Makya doesn't exist in this lifetime? Is he erased from this planet? Because that would be great news!"

"No, but based on things I have learned in the past week, I believe I am the only one who can stop him. I, and I alone, can go after him and stop him. And, I do mean alone."

Josh walked into Brian's office. "That is not happening, not in this lifetime. You are not going after him on your own."

Brick jumped up from his bed and dashed over to greet him, wagging his little stump of a tail. "Hey, boy! Are you keeping Allie out of trouble?"

Shocked to see Josh in the doorway, I walked over and reached up to kiss him on the cheek. "Josh, I thought you weren't coming in until seven?"

Payne interrupted just in time. "I think we need to move this conversation up to the war room. I'm expecting the investigation team to be here in a couple of hours, and we are going to have to give them a report on our findings, which will not be as simple or straightforward as I had hoped it would be."

Chapter 4

A s expected, promptly at seven o'clock, the task force was
ready to begin the day in the war room. This group was
an eclectic ensemble of experts from across the country with
the same common goal: to track down, capture, and lock up
a suspect who had been wreaking havoc across the country
from California to Maine for years.

The Stanford task force members included me and
Detectives Payne and Jake Carpenter. Also from Stanford
were George Pappas, who is like a grandfather to me, my dear
friend, Dakota Channing, Brian from forensics, and Josh
Sullivan, my fiancé, who was there on an as-needed basis
only, as one of Makya's many victims, Dilson Hill, an ex-
convict who did time with Makya, was on the team as well.
Detectives Carl Johnson from New York and Hayln Deere
from Colorado, who had been working previously with the
Stanford police department on this case, were part of the
team, and now they had the addition of the FBI. The group
sent in by them were agents Tracy Davis, Lance Taylor, Noah
Baker, and Adam Rivera. Each of us had up close experience
with the man I knew as Makya. Unfortunately, the cumulation

of all of our experiences came together when I learned I was his end goal all along. The nemesis that I learned about over the past year had been terrorizing women across the entire country with one goal: to find and terminate me before I learned how to stop and destroy him.

As I sat down at the conference table between Dakota and Josh, Brick climbed under the table and curled up at my feet, resting his head against my leg.

As everyone took a seat, Payne stood up and started the meeting. "Good morning, ladies and gentleman. We have a rather unusual and strange development to report today."

I cringed, as I thought, *Here he goes! He's going right to it, and he's going to rip the Band-Aid right off!*

"Cupping his chin in his hand and clearing his throat, he just put it out there. "We have been taking apart something we received from an old auto salvage yard the past couple of days. To make a long story short, it was two things. First, a cube of various materials that were mummified together in an almost perfect rectangle. The second item was a large old trunk. We believe it contained its contents for a substantial amount of time, letting it dry out and form that very cube. When we took the cube apart, we found the contents contained evidence of a homicide, some automatic weapons, and the remains of a male victim. We have yet to determine the cause of death, but we have reason to believe that this murder did not happen locally. That is all I can say for now. We will update you as soon as we have more information."

Much to my surprise, he mentioned nothing about a second body. Could that mean he didn't believe me? Maybe he didn't mention it because, in his reality, there never was a second body, and for him, that is all he could truthfully say.

No, he knew me. I knew he just needed time to let it all sink in so he could wrap his head around it.

Hands started going up immediately as everyone began speaking out of turn.

"Do you think those items and the body are somehow related to the case we are working on?"

"How old was the trunk?"

"What do you mean, 'mummified'? Doesn't that take years?"

Payne raised his hands over his head to stop the mayhem, and when it didn't get quiet, he put two fingers between his lips and let out a blaring whistle. The room became deafeningly silent. "Thank you. We suspect these items could be connected to our case, but let's give forensics a chance to do their job and then look at the facts they present to us. Don't make me sorry I shared this with all of you. I promise I will update you with any new information as soon as I get it."

Payne walked over and stood behind my chair. "I am going to ask Brian and Allie to continue their work down in forensics today. If we need them for anything, we can call them in."

Brian and I got up from our chairs to leave. Brick jumped up and was right behind me at my heels. Josh looked down at a text on his phone and then followed us out the door to catch up with us.

"Allie, I just received a text from Russell Smith at Healthtech Pharmaceuticals. It sounded urgent. I think I should call him back."

Confused, I stopped short. "Have you been in contact with him?"

"No, I haven't!"

"How did he even know you were back?"

"That's a great question! Even more, how did he get my new cell number?"

My cell phone buzzed. It was a message from Claudia. *Allie, call me as soon as you get this!* Holding the phone up to Josh, I dropped my head to my chest like a bowling ball. "I would say this is how he got your number."

The words no sooner left my lips when my cell phone rang. "Hello, Claudia."

"Allie, I am so sorry, but Russell Smith from Healthtech Pharmaceuticals called and asked for Josh. I gave him Josh's new cell number. I hope it's okay! He said he needed to speak with him regarding a matter of the utmost importance. I didn't think he was going back to work for them. Is he considering it?"

"Slow down, Claudia! Look, Josh is going to call him back. Eventually, he would have caught up with him anyway, so don't worry about it. We can talk about this when we get home this evening. Okay?"

"Okay. Tell Josh I'm sorry. I guess I just wasn't thinking."

Josh took the phone from my hand. "Claudia, it's fine. It's not like you gave my number to a total stranger. After all, he was my boss for years. I'm sure there is a good reason he is trying to reach me."

"Thanks, Josh. You're the best!"

Chapter 5

Brian and I went back down to the morgue and continued working with the cadaver and debris on the tables. Hours later, Brian held up a portion of the spine.

Leaning across the metal exam table, looking up straight into my eyes, he started laughing out loud. "Okay, I call uncle."

He laughed so hard it became contagious, and I began chuckling, "And what is that supposed to mean, 'uncle'?"

"You're almost always one step ahead of us. Look, lodged between a couple of these vertebrae is a small chunk of metal, and it's wedged in there pretty tight. Looks like it could be a .38-caliber bullet to me."

Laughing even harder, I took a breath. "Are you kidding? I cheated. I knew the cause of death because I'm the one who shot him. There was no analysis of evidence or science behind it. If I wasn't the person, and pardon the expression, *who done it*, I wouldn't have a clue!"

Brian turned, tapping his index finger on his lips, still smiling. "Well, there is that."

As Brick got up and started pacing the floor, I began cleaning things up. "Hey, Brian, I think that is our cue that we should wrap this up for the day."

Without even looking up, his eyes glued to the computer, he continued typing. "Why don't you and Brick get out of here for the evening? I have a few more notes to log, and I'll be right behind you."

"Are you sure?"

"I'm sure. Besides, it looks like Brick needs a walk outside sooner than later."

"Okay, if you're sure you don't mind. I'll let Payne know I'm leaving. Officer Moretti has been assigned as my security until further notice, so I'm sure he will be waiting for a call to come to pick me up because he is also my transportation."

Taking a deep breath, Brian sighed. "Yeah, I guess I'll have to catch a ride from Payne as well, since he's the one who brought us both in this morning. It's been a damn long day, hasn't it?"

Turning, I tapped him on the shoulder. "Yeah, sorry about that."

"No, you're not."

"Yes, I am!"

Tipping his head, resting his chin between his thumb and forefinger, he smiled. "Ah… Would you do anything differently if you had it to do all over again?"

I had to admit it. He had me there, and I couldn't respond without being dishonest.

He smiled. "Your silence speaks volumes, Allie."

"I suppose it does. Okay, see you in the a.m."

As I headed to the elevator with Brick, I pulled out my cell phone and called Payne. He answered on the first ring.

"Hey, Allie, I was just going to call you. Antonio is on his way to the station to pick you up. He's about five minutes out."

"Great, that should give me just enough time to walk Brick, and then I'll be ready to leave."

Allie, where is Josh? I haven't seen him since he followed you out of the meeting earlier today. I thought it might be a good idea if Antonio followed him back to the Summit as well."

"That would be a great idea, but he left earlier. Someone he worked with from Healthtech Pharmaceuticals contacted him earlier today. It was Russell Smith, a member of the board of directors there. He said he needed to speak with Josh right away regarding something of the utmost importance, whatever that meant."

"Russell Smith? Board of directors at Healthtech? Isn't that where Josh used to work as their lead scientist?"

"Yes. I can't even imagine what they want from him. What's even stranger is how they even knew Josh was back. I'm sure that is one of the first things he asked when they met this afternoon."

"Look, Allie, I'll meet you at the main entrance, walk Brick with you, and wait with you for Antonio. See you in a few minutes."

Chapter 6

Within an hour, Antonio and I were pulling up to the Summit. Henry, the night doorman, met us and opened my door.

"Good evening, Allie. I hope you had a good day."

"Thank you, Henry. It has been an extremely long day, but I'm happy to report that at least it was a productive one. Thanks for asking! How was yours?"

"Considering I work the second shift and my day is just beginning, it is going well. I hope it will continue to go smoothly and be uneventful. A nice, quiet evening would be just fine by me."

Antonio stretched his arms and twisted at the waist, cracking his back as he closed the car door behind him.

"I cringed. "What is it with you guys, always cracking your bones?"

"It feels good. You should try it sometime!"

"That's a hard pass! A stretch is one thing, but I draw the line at bone cracking!"

Antonio passed the keys over to Henry. "We are retiring for the night, and don't have plans to leave the Summit for the rest of the evening."

"Okay, sir. I'll park the car at the end of the drive so it will be accessible just in case you should need it."

As we entered the lobby, Sandy Turner, the night desk manager, called out. "Excuse me. Good evening, Allie."

As I turned in her direction, I couldn't help but notice she was holding a beautifully wrapped package with a perfectly tied red ribbon across the top.

"This arrived for you about an hour ago."

Antonio stepped in front of me. "I'll take that! Thank you, Sandy."

Picking up his cell phone, he immediately called the station. "Hello, Payne. Allie received an unexpected gift here at the Summit. I thought it would be wise for someone more qualified to open it. What do you think?"

After a long pause, he nodded. "I agree. Will do, sir."

Hanging up his phone, and with great care, he placed the package on the floor. Taking a pair of gloves from his pocket and putting them on his hands, he carefully picked up the box again. He turned toward the door. "I am going to go to the parking garage with this and wait for a truck from the station to arrive. They will be here in less than ten minutes. Allie, please wait here with Sandy until we get the all-clear. Sandy, if they find something suspicious, we will need to evacuate the building. In the meantime, could you please cut off the power to the elevator? I need it to be out of service to limit the number of people who have access to the parking garage until they get here. This is probably nothing, but we can't be too careful." With that, he went to the stairwell and walked down to the garage.

Sandy cut the power to the elevators immediately, then turned to me. "Allie, what kind of truck do you think they're sending?"

Reaching down into my purse to grab a piece of gum in an attempt to hide my expression, I squeaked out, "I don't really know. Maybe they're sending the truck from forensics and someone from the lab. Hey, would you like some gum? I know I could use a piece. My mouth is parched."

That part wasn't a lie. My nerves were running on overdrive, and my mouth felt like the Sahara Desert. The problem was, I was sure they were sending a truck from the bomb squad, and, well, I wasn't being completely honest about that. Let's just say that one of us worried and scared was quite enough.

Suddenly I heard Claudia's voice. "Hey, girl, why are you hangin' out down here?"

I looked up to see her and Jake walking into the lobby with large grocery bags under their arms."

"Hi, Claudia, am I glad to see you guys! Here, let me help you with those. You need to put them down over here on the front desk."

"What? Al, are you kidding? I'm starving. Jake and I thought we would surprise you and cook dinner for us tonight."

"Not right now, you aren't!"

Jake dropped his two bags on the front desk. "What's going on, Allie?"

"I'm not sure. Antonio is down in the parking garage. When we got back here a little while ago, there was a gift for me at the front desk. As a cautionary move, Payne sent someone from the station to open the package and ensure it was safe."

I no sooner got the words out when the stairway door opened and Antonio stepped out. He handed me a pair of latex gloves.

"Here Allie, please put these on."

After sliding them on, he handed me an envelope.

"Here, this was in the box. You can read it, but after you do, we need to put it in a plastic bag so I can take it in as evidence.

Opening the envelope, I carefully pulled out the card. There was a picture of one long-stem, red rose, and a blue violet on the front. Inside the card, the verse read: *Roses are red, violets are blue. For you, I will always be true!* There was a line through the poem made with a black felt pen. Taped inside of the card were four dried, black rose petals. A new line was written below the petals: *Roses are dried up and black, but don't be blue, for I will never stop until you are through!*

Spinning to face Claudia, I gasped. "Oh, my God! Remember the first time he came after me at my beach house? He left a vase of black roses on my back deck. Then the night we went to Prescott Park in Portsmouth, New Hampshire, he left that envelope with dried, black rose petals in your car. This guy is one sick son of a bitch!"

Taking a cautious step forward, I reached out. "Antonio, what's in the box?"

He hesitated. "Ah…"

"Antonio? What's in it?"

"It's a snow globe!"

"A snow globe? What the hell? I don't get it. Let me see it!"

"I'm sure you will see the irony when I show it to you, Allie!"

As he pulled it from the box, I slightly stumbled backward. Jake caught me. It was a snow globe, all right, but inside was a replica of my home at the beach. The one where he broke into and left the flowers.

After collecting myself, I turned to Claudia and started pacing the floor. "What did he think I would do? Did he think I would have a meltdown? Did he think this would bring me to my knees? He should know me better by now. He is such a creep! All he's done is infuriate me even more, if that's even possible!"

Claudia grabbed me by the shoulders and spun me around to face her. "Don't you think that is what he might be trying to do? Look, this guy is brilliant. He might want to make you so angry that you become careless or do something reckless. He might want you to make a move without thinking it through. That's how mistakes get made. What did Grandfather always say? Slow on the hunt. Steady on the hunt. Patients on the hunt. No fast moves! Plan and move quietly and carefully, and never move in for the kill until you are sure. You don't want your prey to see you coming or suffering. You want it over quickly and cleanly. This guy needs to face justice, and you need to be smart to bring him in. In this case, it may not be your job to serve him that justice, but to bring him in to face it."

"I'm not sure about bringing him in. It is becoming increasingly clear that I am the only one who can end his reign of terror, and I think he knows that, too. I could see it in his eyes when I traveled back to the early twenties and shot him at my wedding in the Ozarks."

Stunned, Claudia cupped the sides of her face. "What? What are you talking about? Allie, what did I miss?"

"Oops, I'm sorry, Claudia. I forgot I didn't tell you that part yet."

"You're not kidding! I think you have some serious explaining to do, my friend."

Jake took Claudia's hand. "Look, honey, I heard this story today at the station. I think cooking dinner might be better tomorrow night."

"You think? I don't even think I could eat after this little news and fiasco!"

Jake looked up just as Josh walked into the lobby. "Man, am I glad to see you! Why don't you join me, and we can go to George's and get some takeout for supper tonight?"

"What are you talking about? I just got here?"

Jake threw his hand over Josh's shoulder and moved him toward the door. "Trust me, bro, we need to give the girls some space. Allie has some explaining to do. She accidentally let the cat out of the bag prematurely about the events that had happened over the last twenty-four hours. Since Claudia is usually the first to know everything, well, let's just say it didn't go over too well."

Chapter 7

As Jake and Josh left the building, Claudia and I made our way to the apartment. Claudia entered the foyer, dropped her keys in a dish on the entryway table, kicked her shoes off, walked into the great room, and threw herself into one of the recliners. "Okay, Al, spill it!"

"Would you like a glass of wine first?"

"No, stop stalling. Let's get on with it! What the heck is going on? I thought we didn't have any secrets?"

"Look, Claudia, we don't have much time. I have to make this quick because I need to talk to you about my plans beyond this conversation."

Kneeling in front of her, taking her hands in mine, I chuckled nervously. "It's kind of a mess, but the bottom line is, I wasn't able to talk to you about this because it happened when everyone was asleep last night."

A look of confusion came across Claudia's face as her dazed eyes scanned the room.

"Claudia, are you okay?"

It was almost as if she couldn't hear me. A nervous smile crept across her face as she tightened her grip on my hands, swinging them gently from side to side. The movement brought on a familiar sensation, and suddenly I could feel myself starting to slip away again.

Shocked, I broke her grip on my hands and backed away. "Claudia, what are you doing?"

She didn't even flinch.

"Claudia!"

Placing my hands on her cheeks, I turned her face to me and looked deep into her eyes. She was gazing, as if I wasn't even there.

Panic began setting in. "Claudia? Claudia! Claudia, you have got to snap out of it right now! Oh, my God, what is going on?"

As I paced the floor, I remembered the tree of life pendant. I took it off my neck and carefully placed it around hers. As I sat quietly across from her, the light was slowly coming back into her eyes.

"Claudia, thank God! What the heck was that?"

"I know, right? You said it. What the heck just happened?"

"I'm not quite sure, but if I was to venture a guess, you almost time traveled."

"What? Are you kidding? That's great! That means you can take me with you. I can go after Makya with you, right?"

"No, wrong! What did I tell you? I have to do this alone."

"I thought you wanted me to help."

"I do, but—"

"But nothing. How can I help if I can't come with you?"

"Look, Claudia, can I just finish my explanation before Josh and Jake get back? We can talk about the details later."

"Okay, but we aren't done with that conversation!"

"All right, where was I? The bottom line is that last night, I figured out how to travel through time or between dimensions of my own free will. Well, so to speak. I haven't figured it all out yet, but I found myself in another time. It was the early 1920s. Josh, Dakota, Jake, and Makya were all there."

"What? Are you kidding me? How is that possible?"

"It was them from another lifetime. They didn't look the same, but I knew it was them."

"How?"

"Their eyes. I could see it in their eyes."

"Are you kidding me? Their eyes?"

"Yes, our eyes are the windows to our souls. No matter how we look in any time or dimension, our eyes are always recognizable! Look, when I first told Brian and Payne about all this, they thought I was crazy, but I was able to convince them. Don't ask me how. It's too long of a story, but suffice it to say they believe me now."

"Why am I not getting the entire story, Allie?"

"Because I am telling you all I really have time to tell you for now. I can fill in the details later. I need to talk to you about something far more important."

Brick climbed up on the couch beside me and rested his head in my lap. Taking a deep breath, I rested my legs on the coffee table in front of me. "Claudia, you can't tell a single soul what I am about to share with you."

Getting up, she came over and sat on the couch to face me. Rolling her eyes, she let out a groan. "Oh geez, why do I feel like I will regret making that promise?"

"You might, but I know I can count on you to keep a secret. I have to go after Makya, but one thing I know for certain, I need to do it alone."

"Are you kidding me? Josh will never let that happen, and Payne will be furious!"

"Wait, just stop and think about it for a minute. Anyone else will just get in my way. This will take some planning, and God knows all the gifts I can muster up, as well as everything Grandfather has taught me! Makya is far too powerful, and anyone else will just get in the way or be a distraction. It will be hard enough to defend myself, much less protect someone else."

"I don't know, Allie! This really makes me nervous. You should at least take Brick with you! He is well trained and you can trust him to remain quiet when you need him to."

As I stroked the top of his head, Brick snuggled into my lap a little closer. "I plan to. He has become quite the companion for me, and I feel safer having him around. Listen, no one, and I do mean no one, can know about this. Not even Josh, Jake, or Payne. You are the only one. Remember when we went after Makya in the theatre? I had called you and had my phone on mute so you could hear everything that was going on. I plan to use those same types of team techniques this time. Deal?"

"Well, maybe. I still have one concern. We can only use the cell phones when you are in this time. If you go to another time or dimension, we will have to figure out something else."

"You're right, but we'll have to figure that out later. Are you in?"

"So, I'm going along, but I can't go with you when you actually confront him?"

"That's right, that's the deal! Are you in?"

"We are freaking crazy, but you're going to do it with or without my help, right?"

"I'd rather do it with your help. We're a good team, you and me!"

"Okay, I guess it's a deal. I'm in!"

Brick jumped off the couch as the door in the foyer swung open. "Hey, anyone hungry?"

Looking at Claudia, I tipped my head in a questioning manner.

She gave me that disgusted grin and whispered, "I know, I know, mum's the word!"

Chapter 8

Joining Josh and Jake in the kitchen, I offered to get us all something to drink. Iced teas all around, as I set our glasses on the island. "Wow, something smells amazing! I didn't think I was hungry, but the aroma coming from those bags has changed my mind."

Josh smiled. "We got a little of everything. Some assorted finger sandwiches, coleslaw, potato salad, macaroni salad, and chips. So, let's dig in!"

Claudia covered her mouth with both her hands. "Okay, you two, there is enough food here for an army. I think your eyes were bigger than your stomachs."

Jake leaned in and gave her a peck on the cheek. "I think we can make a large dent in this food, Claudia, no problem!"

Sitting at the island, I began filling my plate when something out of the corner of my eye caught my attention. I turned to see Grandfather standing just in front of the refrigerator. As much as I tried to be inconspicuous, Claudia noticed the look on my face and reacted with her wide-eyed, rolling eyes in response. Standing from the island, I shot her my not-now look.

"Hey guys, excuse me for a minute. I will be right back. I think I'll call Mom. Maybe they would like to join us. If not, we can still send some of this food up for them. I'll be right back."

Hoping Grandfather would follow me, I bee-lined to Claudia's art studio. Just as I had hoped, there he was, standing just inside the doorway.

Stunned by his appearance as I entered the room, I blurted, "Grandfather, what is this? Why is your face painted that way?"

"Because, my little bird, you are going to war!"

"No, I'm not!"

He pointed at the window closest to me. "Look at your reflection in the pane?"

As I started toward the window, Claudia walked into the room. "Grandfather?"

Shocked, I spun around. "You can see him? Oh, my God, you can see him!"

"Ah, yes! I can!"

Grandfather's voice grew deeper and his facial expression more serious. "Claudia, please join Allie and gaze into the windowpane, my dear!"

When we stepped over to look at our reflections, we were stunned. I turned to Claudia and then back to the window.

As the color drained from Claudia's face, she cried out in a whisper, "How is that even possible? That's not even us!"

Turning to her, I took both her hands. "Claudia, wait, please let me try to explain. That is our reflection."

"Allie, stop it! You're scaring me! What the heck are you talking about?"

"Okay, wait. Do you trust me?"

"Of course, I do!"

"Then listen. Remember when I went missing because I traveled to another time or dimension and found out that I was Makya's squaw then?"

Claudia let out an audible breath. "Yes, how could I forget? You almost missed my wedding!"

"Well, Makya is not the only one I met there. You were there as well, and you looked just like you do in that reflection."

Turning back to Grandfather, a tear slipped from my eye and fell to my cheek. "I met her during one of my travels."

"Yes, I know, my little bird, but you couldn't stay there. You needed to get back to your true time. Back to George's farmhouse. I am showing you both these versions of yourselves in that lifetime because it is one that you were sisters in."

Claudia was so confused. "I don't understand, Grandfather. Please help me understand. Why are our faces decorated in war paint?"

"As I just told Allie, you are going to war! This was always meant to be. In this life, I have trained you both well. Do you remember your lessons? This is your destiny. You may not be sisters by blood in this lifetime, but you were in many other lifetimes.

"Allie, you are no longer my little bird, as now you soar with the eagles. Claudia, you are the powerful bird that gives your sister steadiness. You keep her from becoming too serious and, at times, too impulsive. You are always in her life to protect her heart. Together, you support and keep each other balanced."

Grandfather extended his hand and pointed to the key and pendent that now hung around Claudia's neck. There is a second tree of life. One that has an owl, the bird of wisdom, weaved into it. The key you wear on your neck will unlock its hiding place. That pendant belongs to you, Claudia. Many lifetimes ago, the two of you were separated from each other. Your pendants were seized by Makya's great-great-grandfather and hidden from us for many generations. The two of you are great warriors, and when you stand together and are wearing the pendants, you are safe to travel anywhere you need to, knowing you will never be lost and always return to your true time and destiny.

"Allie, you were within mere feet of it the day before Claudia's wedding. That key will unlock the space where you will find the pendant. It hangs on a string named C. You have only to find the other pendent and while you both wear them on your necks, together you will have the wisdom to locate and stop Makya once and for all, with no fear."

Looking back at my reflection in the windowpane, I stood a little taller.

When Claudia looked up and caught my gaze in the mirror, tears were streaming down her face. She turned and as she scanned the room. "Grandfather, he's gone! What are we supposed to do now?"

Using my sleeve to wipe the tears from her face, I whispered, "Claudia, you have to pull yourself together. We can't be too much longer. Josh and Jake are going to wonder what's going on."

I no sooner got the words out before I heard Josh's voice. "Hey Al, are your mom and Guile coming down?"

"Hold on, Josh, we'll be right there!"

Luckily, I reached my mom right away. They were too tired to join us, but said they would love some food. I told them we would bring some up to them after we ate.

Claudia moved across the room and stood directly in front of me. "Now what?"

"Look, why don't you go to the bathroom, rinse off your face and meet me back at the island? I'll tell Jake you'll be right in to join us. Take a minute to pull yourself together. I think we need a girl's day off tomorrow, don't you?"

"What? Are you kidding? Who feels like a girl's day off at a time like this?"

"We're not really going to have a girl's day. That's just an excuse! We need a day off to make plans, but we can't tell them that."

"Really, Allie, do you think they are going to buy that? You're right in the middle of that investigation and autopsy with Brian."

"Well, that's the best I've got. We'll just have to wing it."

Chapter 9

Making my way back to the kitchen, I sat at the island and leaned in and kissed Josh on the cheek. "Mom and Guile are already settled in for the night, but they haven't eaten yet. I told them we would bring them some food up shortly."

He laughed. "I thought you got lost in there. I was ready to send in a rescue team."

Claudia walked back in and sat down at the island, looking as if nothing had even happened. "Very funny!"

Changing the subject, I turned to Josh. "Hey, honey, I meant to ask you earlier, what did Russell Smith want with you today? Whatever possessed him to reach out to you? As far as we knew, he didn't even know you were back. It's been on my mind all day. I kept thinking you would call me at some point to fill me in."

"You're right. I'm sorry, Allie. It wasn't as mysterious as I thought. They were getting close to releasing a new generic version of a pharmaceutical I had initially released. They hoped that by some long shot, I might be back and called the station to see. Russell was actually calling to speak to you, but whoever answered the phone started a conversation with him. When he told them the reason for his call, clearly without thinking, they let the cat out of the bag. Anyway, when they couldn't reach me there, he tried the apartment and contacted Claudia. I don't think Payne found out about it until just before he left the station, but I'm sure we will hear about it tomorrow."

Smirking, I rolled my eyes. "I'm sure you're right, because I saw him when I was leaving today and he didn't mention it to me. If he knew then, he would not have been able to hold back; he would have been exploding, especially because they are trying to keep this as much on the down-low as possible. I am sure you will all hear about it tomorrow."

"Yeah, you're right! I'm sure we will. In fact, it will probably be one of the first things he will mention in our morning meeting."

"Ah…ya, about that. Claudia and I have some things to do tomorrow. I think I won't be going to the station."

Josh and Jake turned their heads and, in unison, replied, "What?"

Claudia quickly interjected and nervously began babbling, as only she could do. "Yeah, I talked Allie into taking the day off to start planning her wedding. I mean, not that you have picked a date or anything. It's just that there has been a lot of stress in her life. You know, I thought she could use a little distraction, something positive for a change. Look, since it hasn't been that long since our wedding and everything is still fresh in my mind, I thought we should start planning yours now, ya know? We can go on the Internet, look at dresses, venues, cakes, and all that stuff. Don't you think that's a great idea? We can just have a relaxing no business, all-girl, fun kind of day."

Reaching under the counter, I grabbed Claudia's knee and squeezed to get her attention. When she finally stopped, I turned to her. "Claudia, I'm sure they don't need to hear all the boring details that we women go through to plan our weddings."

Jake turned to Josh. "That sounds like a plan, right Josh?"

Josh reached out, gently tucking a loose strand of hair behind my ear, and smiled. "Is that what you want to do, Allie?"

I hated to lie to him. I knew the thought of my making our wedding plans would really make him happy, but this was so deceitful.

Praying he wouldn't think it was forced, I smiled. "Yes, of course."

"Well then, nothing on this Earth would make me happier!"

After eating, I started packing up some food for Mom and Guile. "Hey, guys, do you think you could take this food upstairs for us while we clean up?"

Jake turned. "Sure thing! Hey, let's make a plate for Antonio. I'm sure he's hungry."

While Josh and Jake went to deliver the food, Claudia and I quickly cleaned up the dishes and put the rest of the food away.

Closing the refrigerator door, I turned and took a deep breath. A lump was swelling up in my throat. "I really hate lying to Josh and Jake!"

Claudia wiped down the island, looked up, rolling her eyes as she pursed and smacked her lips. "Do you think we dare tell them what we are really planning?"

"Are you kidding? They would never let us out of their sight." Brick strolled over, rested his chin on my leg, looked up at me, and whined.

"What is it, boy?"

Claudia laughed. "Sometimes I feel like he knows exactly what we're talking about. It's just crazy!"

"I know, right?"

"Look, Allie, I think I am going to ask Jake to go to bed early this evening. Like maybe, as soon as they get back from delivering the food to your mom and Guile."

"I was thinking the same thing. It might be the last time for a while we get to have some really quality bedtime with them, if you know what I mean."

A few minutes later, Josh and Jake came through the door. Claudia and I laughed as Brick greeted them with his leash hanging out of his jowls. Reaching down, Josh took the leash. "Okay, boy, I can take a hint."

Shaking his head in a questioning manner, Jake smirked. "If you ask me, that was more than a hint. That was a direct request. Come on, I'll join you."

As I turned to the foyer, I called out, "Hey, guys, don't be too long! Claudia and I are going to bed a little early and, well, you wouldn't want us to fall asleep! I can't speak for her, but I know I have plans!"

Jake opened the door for Josh. "Believe me, this will be the fastest walk we have ever taken. See you in a few."

Chapter 10

Within ten minutes, Josh come through the bedroom door. Poking my head out from around the corner of the walk-in closet, I teased, "Hey, honey, why don't you shower and make yourself comfortable? I'll be right with you."

He showered and climbed into bed in record time. When I emerged from the closet, I was wearing long black silk stockings suspended by a black corset laced up the front with a thin red ribbon. It was hidden just slightly under a thin silk negligee that flowed down to my hips, and was closed only at my neck by a second red bow.

Pulling the ribbon at the neck of the negligee, I let it drop to the floor. "Josh, are you sure you want to stay in that bed right now?"

Tongue-tied, he sat there, struggling for the words. Dragging himself across the bed, he stood, stared at me, and finally found his voice. "Oh, God, you are a sight to behold, Allie. What did I ever do to deserve being this happy?"

"Honey, I could ask the same!"

He took one step toward me and stopped.

I smirked. "I won't bite, you know."

Moving closer, he brushed my hair back behind my shoulders. "I just want to take my time and enjoy each and every moment."

Those familiar sensations began coursing through my body as my breath grew slower and deeper. "Josh, I—"

As he covered my lips with his, I thought he might devour me. Backing me up slowly, he gently sat me down on the bed and dropped to his knees.

Gazing deeply into my eyes, he took hold of the first clip on my stockings. "May I?"

"Oh yes, please!"

As he gently released my stockings, one clip at a time, I leaned back, bracing myself on the bed with my arms, as the silk stockings slid gently down one leg at a time. Josh reached up and pulled my arms out from under me, and I fell back on the bed. Reaching up, he pulled on one of the tails of the ribbon at the top of my corset, releasing the bow. Hovering over me on his hands and knees, he pulled the ribbon through the eyelets of the corset one at a time, until it fell away from my body, exposing my bare skin.

Lifting my naked form off the bed, he dragged back the covers, lay me back down, engulfing me with his entire body as once again I was swallowed up by that amazing and familiar sensation as we became one in an overture of ecstasy.

Time seemed to stand still as we lay there, sweat-drenched and in sheer exhaustion. Josh stretched and drew the down comforter up over us as he rolled in my direction. Reaching over, he pulled the hair back from my face and tucked it behind my ear, hesitating before he spoke. "Allie, sometimes you scare me."

Running my index finger softly down his nose and over his lips, I took a deep breath. "Why, whatever do you mean by that, Mr. Sullivan? How could a black belt like you be afraid of me?"

"I'm serious, Allie. I'm worried that you are going to go off on your own and do something crazy."

"Josh, let's not ruin this wonderful moment talking about Makya. Can't we just let it go for tonight?"

His answer became apparent when he wrapped his arms around me, catapulting us back into a second blissful encounter that would drain us both and send us off to a deeply restful sleep that would last through the entire night.

We slept so soundly and didn't stir all night until we woke to the blaring of the alarm clock at six o'clock. Josh reached over me to turn it off and then curled up next to me. "Do we really have to get up? Maybe I could stay home today, too. I could always help you and Claudia with the wedding plans. After all, it's my wedding, too."

I lay there, stunned. That was the last thing I expected to come out of his mouth! I had to think quickly!

Turning to face him, I gave him a gentle kiss. "You can't help with these plans! We might pick out my dress today, and it's bad luck for the groom to see the bride's dress before the wedding! Besides, you and Jake will have your day together picking out your tuxes."

Josh burst out laughing. "Oh, I just can't wait!"

"And what is that supposed to mean?"

"Well, let me think about that. You and Claudia get to listen to amazing bands, taste-test great foods, and decadent cakes, but Jake and I get to pick out our tuxes. Hmm, I think the two of you get the better end of that deal!"

"I'll tell you what. I'll make you a promise. When it's time to do those things, we'll invite you guys to go with us! Deal?"

"Deal!"

Chapter 11

The next morning, while Josh showered, I slid on my robe and headed into the kitchen, where I found Jake sitting at the island with a cup of coffee in hand, reading the *Stanford News*.

"Good morning, Jake. Is Claudia up yet?"

"No, I let her sleep this morning because I knew the two of you had your own plans today. Speaking of that, have you called Payne to let him know you plan to take a day off?"

"No, I'm going to make that call after I have my coffee. Believe me, I'm not looking forward to having that conversation with him."

"Oh, I don't know. I think Payne might just surprise you. He would probably agree that you need to take a day off."

I turned from the counter to find Josh standing in the doorway, grinning from ear to ear. He turned to Jake. "So, my friend, how did you and Claudia sleep last night?"

"Like a rock! And the two of you?"

Josh smirked. "You could say we slept from sheer exhaustion."

I piped in. "Okay, that's enough sharing, you two!"

Getting up from his seat, Jake handed the newspaper to Josh. "Do you want to read this before we head out this morning? It looks like you'll be riding to the station with me today, buddy. Antonio will have to stay here with Claudia and Allie."

"Sure thing. What time do you want to head out?"

"How about six forty-five? That will get us to the station by seven."

"Six forty-five it is. I'll be ready!"

Walking into the kitchen, Claudia planted a kiss on Jake's cheek. "Well, good morning, you guys. Did I miss anything this morning?"

Scooping her up in his arms, he gave her a huge bear hug. "No, not a thing. Josh and I were just talking about heading out to the station soon. Are you girls cooking tonight or should we pick up something?"

Claudia grunted. "Down, boy, let go. I can hardly breath! I think we still have enough food leftover from last night, if we don't mind leftovers."

Pulling a bowl of fruit from the refrigerator, I agreed. "Sounds like a plan to me."

Right on Cue, at six forty-five, Josh and Jake were out the door and on their way to the station. As soon as they walked out the door, I sat down at the island, took a deep breath, and then rested my head on the counter. "God, Claudia, we haven't even got a plan yet, and I am already exhausted. I don't even know where we should start."

Claudia grabbed a pad of paper and sat down next to me at the island. "Grandfather made it pretty clear. He said we needed to find the second tree of life, the one that belongs to me. It sounded like we needed both pendants to go up against Makya. Don't you think that is as good a place as any to start?"

"Yes, you're absolutely right, but it's not that simple. Pardon my French, but even if we can figure out where to look for the pendant, how the hell are we going to get out of here? We have surveillance twenty-four-seven."

"Well, that's what we are going to figure out. Why don't you give Payne a call? Tell him you aren't coming in today because we are going to start planning your wedding. That will give you a good reason to be busy at least today, or maybe even a second day if we need it, right? While you do that, I'll make Antonio a coffee and offer him something to eat. Then we can shower before we settle into the great room with a calendar and notepad to figure out what our first move will be. We should probably work on something related to the wedding as well, just so we can show Josh and Jake that we did."

Chapter 12

When I made it back to the great room, Claudia was there waiting. "Wow, how did you get ready so fast?"

"I had an excellent incentive. We don't have much time. I think I have everything we need to get started. I even made us a tall pitcher of iced water with fresh fruit. So how did your call to Payne go?"

"Much better than I could have imagined. He was terrific about it. In fact, he told me to take as much time as I needed. However, he did have one stipulation."

"What was that? Wait, let me guess! He wants you to be on call in case they need you."

"Yes, but well, I think that was a great compromise. Don't you?"

"I guess so."

"So, let's get to work."

Claudia grabbed my hand to stop me from pacing the floor. "Can you please sit down Allie?"

"Sorry, I can't. I do some of my best thinking when I'm moving around."

"Well, I find it distracting. Do you think we could find a happy medium?"

Giving in, I took a seat at the table. Looking down, I lifted the chain around my neck.

"Remember what Grandfather told us? He said the day before your wedding, I was within feet of your pendant, and this key will unlock whatever container or location your pendant is in."

Sinking into deep thought, Claudia rolled her eyes. "Yeah, but I don't understand the rest of it. He said it will be hung on a string name C?"

I poured a glass of water from the pitcher Claudia had made. "Wow, this is really good?"

To get my attention back, Claudia waved her hands in my face. "Earth to Allie, let's stay focused!"

Standing, I walked to the window on the other side of the room and turned. "Sorry. Okay, first things first. I wasn't even here in this time the day before your wedding. I was at my own wedding in the 1920s. That's right, I was at my wedding to James in the Ozarks. So, the pendant had to be there somewhere. It could have been in the cabin, the church, or even that old Model-T Ford."

"Allie, What? You never told me about a Model-T Ford. That's so cool!"

"That's it, Claudia. We need to go to that old lodge at the Ozarks in Missouri."

"Standing, she stepped in front of me and stopped me in my tracks. Are you crazy? That old hunting lodge is probably not even there anymore. They probably tore it down years ago."

Raising my eyebrows, I tipped my head. "Do you have a better idea?"

"Well, no, if you recall, I wasn't with you that day. Remember, I was frantically waiting for you to come home in time for my wedding? You know, the one that was happening in the here and now?"

"Yes, but I made it back in time, right? You can't hold that against me forever. Anyway, I know the cabin is still there. It's been in my family for years!"

The room went silent. We both just stood there gawking at each other. Finally, Claudia broke the silence. "So, Missouri is where we start this trek, but then what?"

We were both so engulfed in our conversation; we didn't even see Antonio enter the great room. "Okay, you two, what are you up to? No one is going to Missouri! Not on my watch, you aren't."

Spinning around, I recovered quickly. "No, you're right. No one is going to Missouri now. Didn't we tell you we took today off to plan Josh and my nuptials? We were thinking of a destination wedding. My family has an old hunting lodge there. I've thought that it might make a great place to spend our honeymoon."

Antonio's face twisted as though he was in pain, and letting out an audible groan, he offered his opinion. "Well, if you like mosquitoes, flies, and smokey fires, I guess that's for you. As for me, I'll trade that for a hut somewhere on the beach in the Caribbean any day."

Turning to leave the room, he raised his hand. "I'll leave you two to your planning. I'm going to use the restroom, but I need to get back to work. Could I bother you for another cup of coffee?"

As he left the room, I turned to Claudia and sighed with relief. "Sure, I'll bring one right out to you."

When I returned from delivering Antonio's coffee, Claudia had her nose planted in her laptop. "Hey, Allie, we need to visit the bridal shop so you can try on some wedding gowns."

I took a seat next to her on the couch and started whispering, "What are you talking about? When I left the room five minutes ago, we were mulling over the possibility of going to Missouri, and now you are talking about picking out my wedding dress!"

Shifting in her seat to face me, Claudia gave me her no-duh expression. "How do you suppose we are going to shed that appendage that follows us everywhere we go?"

"What?"

"Think about it, Allie. We have to be in a place where Antonio can't shadow us. Like in a dressing room at the bridal shop?"

"Oh... Yeah! Right! So today, we will plan our travel itinerary, as well as my wedding dress shopping, both of which need to happen tomorrow!"

"Correct! And if we plan this right, we can get everything ready today. For instance, we can't use credit cards while traveling, or they can track us."

"That's true. It will be hard to travel without credit cards for sure, but you're right. That means we'll need to make a huge withdrawal from the bank before leaving. You know what else? We won't be able to use our cell phones either. They'll be able to trace them. What about burner phones?"

"I don't know, Allie. I think we can use them if we're cautious. Keeping them turned off and only using them when we're apart or for emergencies. I have heard once you use them, they can be traced."

"Maybe we get four of them, so we use the first two and then ditch them if we need to, and then we have a backup."

"That could work!"

"As for packing, we won't be able to leave with much. I would say, probably the clothes we wear and anything we can fit in the largest handbags we own. As for transportation, we will need to use some sort of public transport that doesn't require a credit card, like a bus."

"Well, if we travel by bus or train, I'm pretty confident we won't be able to take Brick."

"Crap, I hadn't thought of that. You're right, we'll have to drive, but if we take one of our cars, they will track us by simply putting out an APB. I have a better idea. My dad has already headed home and has parked his SUV in storage over in Portsmouth. He has given me some keys, and it's not unusual for me to pick the car up from time to time to use it. We can drive that car, and hopefully, we will be long gone by the time they can figure out we have it."

"Man, Claudia, you sound like you have done this before."

"No, but to be honest, I lay awake all night thinking about it. We don't have much time to plan this, and I do think the sooner we leave, the better. That way, before anyone has a chance to suspect anything, we'll already be long gone."

Leaning forward, I grabbed a pad of paper off the coffee table. "Okay, let's get to it and make a list of what we absolutely need to take with us. First, we will need some gear and warm and comfortable clothes to blend into any landscape. Since we're starting in the Ozarks, I feel relatively certain that we may need to track Makya through some tough terrain."

"Look, Allie, I know we're going to need much more than we can leave this apartment with. Don't you think it makes more sense to buy what we need in the way of gear and clothing when we get there?"

"You're right. Good thinking. We'll have to make sure we withdraw enough cash for everything! I will, however, make sure I have my handgun, and we should both carry some mace."

"Al, wait. Don't you think you should get the ancestral box? I mean, I know the box won't fit in anything we are carrying, but maybe you should go through it and see if there is anything in it you feel compelled to take?"

"You're absolutely right! I wonder if Dakota has left for the station yet."

Picking up my cell, I dialed his number. Answering on the third ring, he chimed in, "Hey, good morning, Allie! I heard you weren't coming into the station today."

Rolling my eyes at Claudia, trying desperately to sound sincere, I blurted out, "Good morning to you, too, Dakota. No, I'm taking a couple of days off. Claudia and I are going to start planning Josh and my wedding."

"Well then, what can I do for you? Do you need my limo that day?"

"Sure, that would be great! We were hoping you would offer!"

"Sure thing, Allie! I bet we could even get Henry to drive for the wedding. Is that all you needed?"

"Ah…no, not exactly!"

"What is it then?"

"When you get home this evening, could you bring Grandfather's ancestral box down to Claudia's apartment? I do appreciate you keeping it safe, but I would like to explore its contents again."

"Of course!"

"Thank you, Dakota. See you then."

As soon as I hung up, Claudia bounced off the couch and whispered, "I need to see if I can get us an appointment at the Boutique Leslie Bridal shop for tomorrow afternoon."

"Wait, am I really going to pick out my bridal gown tomorrow?"

"You absolutely are!"

"OMG, I just love that shop. They have the most fantastic selection of dresses!"

"Yes, they do, and just wait until you meet Danielle. She's one of the owners and is just amazing!"

Claudia made a call and got us an appointment the next day at three-thirty, and then we each spent some time packing and preparing for the great escape.

When I finished packing, I slipped over to Claudia's room. "Okay, sometime between now and tomorrow afternoon, we need to find an excuse to go to the bank so we can each make a rather sizable withdrawal."

"You're right, and we need to plan our route to the Ozarks. It might be wise to go old school and pick up some paper maps to use. Then there is that other little detail. We need to pick up those burner phones."

A little overwhelmed with the thought of everything we would need to do without Antonio knowing, I sat down on Claudia's bed. "I don't know if we can get all this accomplished in twenty-four hours. Maybe we should take another day?"

"No, Allie! We need to move on this tomorrow! The longer we wait, the more opportunity there is for us to get caught. Look, on our way to the Bridal Boutique, we can ask Antonio to take us to the bank at the mall. After all, you will need a deposit for your dress."

"But, Claudia, what about the burner phones?"

"I don't know. Maybe we can go to one of those phone kiosks with the excuse that you need a new cover for your cell phone. Then you can buy the burner phones while I distract Antonio long enough for you to make the purchase."

"I don't know. Once we're gone, and they know we don't have our phones, it's a short leap to the burner phone idea. Antonio will put two and two together really quickly, and they will trace what we purchased at the kiosk. You make it sound so easy, but I don't know Claudia!"

"Okay, so we will get the burner phones once we are on the road, and we'll use cash. Trust me, Al! It's like grandfather said, I am the strong bird that gives you steadiness, the one who keeps you from becoming too serious or impulsive. And I am always the one who keeps you on track! It's my job to protect your heart, and together we keep each other well balanced."

Chapter 13

That evening, when Josh and Jake got home from the station, Claudia and I already had dinner on the table. The clicking of Brick's claws on the floor in the foyer as he pranced around, waiting for Josh to get through the door, alerted us they were home.

I headed into the hall to meet Josh as he reached down to greet Brick. "Okay, boy, where's Allie?"

"I'm right here. Welcome home, you two."

Jake turned as Claudia entered the foyer. "Hey, honey, is dinner ready? We're famished."

"We're having leftovers, remember? We still have enough to feed a small army. How about you, Antonio? Could you use something to eat?"

"Sure thing! That would be great. Payne is coming over to relieve me for a while so I can go home, take a shower, and get a few hours' sleep."

He no sooner got the words out when his cell phone went off. Looking down to read a text, he sighed. "It's Payne, and he's on his way up now. If you don't mind, I think I'll skip dinner. I'll grab something to eat at my apartment. The sooner

I get to bed, the better. I need to be here to relieve Payne early tomorrow morning."

Payne arrived and took Antonio's post in the foyer within a few minutes. As he took a seat, I asked, "Payne, are you hungry? We're about to have dinner. It's just leftovers from our meal last night, but I could make you a plate."

"Thank you, Allie, but I grabbed a bite to eat before I came. I'll be fine."

Pulling a folder out from under his arm, he chuckled. "I have a cold case file I need to review. This morning, there was an incident, and it jogged my memory about a case we dealt with three years ago. One that never really set well with me."

"What kind of incident?"

"It was a robbery, gone wrong. We apprehended four suspects, but two were shot at the scene and died in the ambulance on the way to the hospital. There was something else that caught my attention about the two cases. Well, actually, there was a common thread to a third case. It was the kidnapping of Jennie Slater."

What? Are you kidding? How did you tie a cold case to a recent robbery and Jennie's kidnapping?"

"Remember when we found Jennie tied to a pillar under the dock at Old Orchard Beach? The restraints they used were mere strips of material that were braided together to form some sort of makeshift rope."

Payne pulled three plastic bags from his pocket and held them up one at a time. "This bag contains the ties from Jennie's abduction. This second one was from the robbery three years ago, and the third is from this morning. We arrested a young man for shoplifting, and low and behold, he had a third piece of braided cloth in his possession."

"Payne, OMG, this might not be a good time for me to be taking any days off!"

"Nonsense. There is always going to be a case for us to solve. If you stayed at work, every time something new came up, you would never get a break, much less have time to plan your wedding or even get married! Look, go have dinner, and forget about all this. When you come back to work, I'll bring you up to speed."

"But, Payne—"

"Allie, no buts about it! Go enjoy your dinner!"

Leaving the foyer in protest, I went to the kitchen and sat down at the island with the others. "Okay, let's dig in!"

As we began eating, the inevitable happened. Josh reached over, took my hand, and asked, "So, you two, how are the wedding plans going?"

Claudia got up immediately, tucked tail, and excused herself. "Hey, Al, I have to use the restroom. Why don't you fill the guys in on our day? I'll be right back!"

I shot her a look that did not go unnoticed by Josh. He rolled his eyes at Jake. "What do you think, because I believe they're up to something? Something they don't want us to know about."

Tapping Josh on the back, Jake laughed. "Oh, come on, Josh, you know they are up to something! They are working on those oh-so-secret wedding arrangements. Claudia guarded our wedding day plans like Fort Knox, and I was only informed on a need-to-know basis! Believe me, I know what I'm talking about! I have already been down this road."

I began to panic, but Claudia saved me as she walked out of the room with her tireless sense of humor that never failed. "Oh, Allie, they always think we are up to something!"

My nervousness came down a few notches as Jake bantered with Josh, teasing me until Claudia returned.

Entering the room, she playfully whispered, just loud enough for them to both hear, "So, Allie, should we let them know about our secret plans to run away?"

I couldn't believe what had just come out of her mouth! "What, Claudia?"

My shocked reaction was just what she wanted, and she continued. "Yes, we are planning a great escape. Tomorrow, we will leave this apartment with Antonio to visit the Boutique Leslie Bridal shop in Dover, New Hampshire. You know, Jake, where I bought my gown? After that, we are off to look at a couple of venues. Maybe the two of you would like to meet us and help us pick out a hall for the reception?"

The guys were in overload! She was brilliant because the last thing they wanted to do was visit venues and get involved with that part of the planning.

Jake laughed. "No, I think we'll sit this one out. What do you say, Josh?"

"Yes, I am perfectly fine with that. Besides, Allie, didn't you say I couldn't go anywhere near your dress before the wedding?"

Just in time to break up the conversation, Dakota walked into the kitchen with the ancestral box. "I hope you don't mind the intrusion. Payne let me in."

Jake stood. "No, of course not. Come in! How about something to drink? A beer, perhaps?"

"No, thank you. I can only stay a few minutes. I'm on my way out. I have a previous engagement this evening."

Claudia pursed her lips, trying not to laugh. "Do tell! And who is this previous engagement with? Is it perhaps a date with someone we know? Maybe someone we don't know?"

Dakota rolled his eyes, contemplating his answer. "I think I will plead the fifth for now."

Turning to Claudia, I smiled. "So, a hah, it must be a date!"

Chapter 14

After Josh and Jake headed to the station the following day, we sat down at the island in the kitchen with the ancestral box.

"Okay, Claudia, there is no time like the present." Opening the lid, I carefully lifted different objects up, one at a time. My frustration growing, I looked up at Claudia. "I'm not even sure what I am looking for. How am I to know what I might need in here while we're away?"

Claudia placed her hand on the first tray and lifted it out, setting it off to the side. "Well, we both agree we can't get out of here tomorrow with this entire box. Isn't there anything that is speaking to you?

The minute the words left her mouth, we both looked up and laughed.

"Okay! Not literally speaking to you! You know what I meant. There must be something here that is giving you some sort of vibe. Something that resonates with you. You have to take whatever you think we might need."

A beautiful, unique belt and buckle caught my eye as I stared down at the second tray. I lifted and began unrolling it.

The leather was old, but had been lovingly cared for. Clearly, someone had been conditioning it through the years to keep it soft and supple. It was adorned with beautiful beaded artwork, sewn in a pattern that depicted several eagles flying in one direction toward the buckle. The buckle had a plate-style frame fashioned around a buffalo-head nickel, and the prong fastener was a thin arrow.

Lifting it from the box, there was a familiarity. "This is it, Claudia! I don't know why, but this is definitely it!"

I placed the belt carefully on the counter and stacked the shelves back into the ancestral box. As I was closing the lid, it vibrated in my hand and shot up my arm, causing me to release it. Leaning over, I cautiously took hold of the lid again, closed my eyes, and lifted it open. I hesitated before I spoke and then blurted out, "Maybe not."

Standing to look down into the box, Claudia nervously bit her lip. "What does that mean, 'maybe not'? What just happened?"

"I don't know, but somehow this box was objecting to my closing the lid. There must be something more I might need."

Once again, I took the shelves out one at a time until I reached the bottom of the box. Leaning back, I sat akimbo in my chair. "I don't get it! Nothing else in this box stands out! What am I missing?"

I continued looking through everything in the box, picking up and examining every object as carefully as possible.

"Al, think about what grandfather said. We're going to war. What might we need in this box? How about the arrowheads?"

"Those won't be of much use if we have no way to use them. It's not like we can attach them to an arrow and then walk out of here this afternoon with bows and arrows."

"No, but I think I would take them out of the box and see what happens. What have you got to lose?"

Removing the six arrowheads, I attempted closing the box one more time. "I think you might be right, Claudia. I felt nothing this time."

Turning to the Keurig, she gloated. "Well, what do you know? I guess that's it then. How about another coffee?"

"You know you can be incorrigible, right?"

"I know, but when you're right, you're right! Come on, let's sit and go over our plans one more time. I think we need to make sure we haven't forgotten anything."

As we both sat at the island, it was eerily quiet. Neither of us spoke until Claudia broke the silence. "Al, are you having second thoughts about all of this?"

"No, not at all!"

"Well, what's going on in that head of yours? I can see the wheels turning!"

Leaning to one side, I rested my head on my hand. "Something that Payne told me last night is bothering me. Remember, Claudia? He hired me to work on cold cases? The truth is, he believes that this shoplifting incident that happened yesterday morning is somehow connected to a robbery he worked on three years ago, as well as the kidnapping of Jennie Slater. I feel like he needs me on this cold case he's currently investigating, but I won't be around to help, and he doesn't even know that. I guess I'm feeling a little guilty."

"Well then, Allie, the sooner we get out of here and put this whole thing to rest with Makya, the sooner you can do your new job with Payne, without distraction, right?"

"I guess so."

"Alrighty then! Look, another thing. Last night, I was mulling this over in my head. Do you think we should leave a note for Josh and Jake when we leave today? I mean, don't you think it might help put their minds at ease?"

"At ease? Ah, no, but I think we should leave a note. They're going to be furious with us for just taking off like this. I know Josh thinks it's his job to help and keep me safe in this world, but you and I both know that isn't the case."

Claudia chuckled. "I think the operative words here are *safe in this world*. Until we put an end to Makya's reign of terror in any world, no one is safe!"

We spent the rest of the morning composing notes to Jake and Josh. It was a tough ordeal, but we finally got through it. At two o'clock, we showered and got ready for our departure to the shop and, unbeknown to anyone else, our trip. I put Brick's leash on him, picked up my bag, and headed toward the door with Claudia. As we entered the foyer, Antonio stood.

"Well, looks like you two are all ready for your afternoon out!" He looked down at his cell phone. "Aren't we leaving a little early? I mean, you said your appointment at the boutique wasn't until three-thirty, right?"

Claudia chimed in. "Yes, but you know how it is. Besides, we need to make a stop at the mall to go by the bank."

Sliding on his jacket, Antonio pulled his keys from his pocket. "Alright then, the mall it is! Listen, you two, we need to stay together when we stop anywhere. No wandering off without me, right?"

We answered in unison. "Right!"

At the mall, we successfully made our withdrawals and, sliding them into our bags, we headed out.

Chapter 15

We arrived at the boutique promptly at three-thirty that afternoon. Danielle greeted us at the shop entrance. Gazing down at Brick, she smiled. "Well, well, who is this fine fellow?"

Once again, Claudia thought fast on her feet. "his is Brick! I hope you don't mind. He is Allie's support dog."

I didn't know how she pulled this stuff out of thin air, but I just joined in., "Yes, this is Brick. I never go anywhere without him. We should have mentioned him when we made our appointment yesterday."

To quickly move the conversation in a different direction, I turned. "And this is Antonio. He is our driver. Do you mind if he sits here in the shop while we try on dresses?"

Raising his arm to object, Claudia quickly interrupted him. "Antonio, I'm sure you won't mind waiting here. We will need a little privacy in the dressing room. It will make it easier for Allie to slip in and out of different gowns."

Danielle finally got a word in edgewise. "Sure, have a seat, Antonio. Can I get you a coffee, water, or a soft drink?"

"A coffee would be great!"

As the three of us left the front of the shop, Danielle turned to her assistant. "Ellen, could you please get this fine young gentleman a coffee?"

When we got to the dressing room, Brick quickly made himself at home, jumping up on the pedestal used for measuring and making alterations. He circled a few times, lay down, and then looked up at us as if to say, *Okay, ladies, take your time. I'll be right here waiting!*

Danielle couldn't help but chuckle a little. "He certainly is a good boy and quite mannerly!

Turning back to Claudia, she asked, "So, how was your wedding?"

"It was just amazing!"

Taking a cautious breath, she looked in my direction. "Allie, did you make it home in time to stand up for Claudia on that day?"

"Yes, I did. I got back the night before. I have to say the gown she chose for me was amazing, and it fit perfectly!"

Danielle pointed to a selection of dresses on a rack directly behind her. "I'm delighted to hear that. Because we knew your dress size before you arrived this afternoon, I pulled a few gowns for you to look at."

Claudia moved to the rack and began swooning. "Allie, just look at these dresses. Which one do you want to try on first?"

Dancing over to join her, I began swaying back and forth. "Oh, I don't know, let's try them all!"

Lifting a dress from the middle of the rack, I pressed it against my body and spun around. "Let's start with this one!"

Grinning, Danielle took the dress. "That's a great place to start. Follow me."

Pulling back a drape on the side of the dressing room, Danielle asked, "Would you like some help getting into the gown?"

"That would be great!"

Less than five minutes later, I stepped out from behind the curtain. "So, what do you think, Claudia?"

"Oh, my God, Allie, that dress is just stunning! You look like you just stepped out of a fairy tale, or a magazine or something! That dress is so amazing!"

"I know. I just love this gown. I'm not sure if I even need to try anything else on!"

Standing behind me, Claudia peeked over my shoulder and stared at us both in the mirror. "It's beautiful, but don't you think you should make sure that this is the one? You should at least try on a couple more styles."

"I don't know, Claudia. I think when you know, you know. Right, Danielle?"

"Well, it's hard to disagree with that, but I do have one more thing to add to this ensemble that I think will make it perfect. Wait right here. I'll be right back."

When Danielle stepped out, Claudia spun me around, pointing to the opposite side of the room. "Allie, behind that desk and partition is a door that no one knows about. It leads to the cellar and a back entrance. That's how we will get out of here unnoticed."

"What? If no one knows about it, how did you discover it?"

"She showed it to me when I was here to pick out my wedding gown. We were kind of joking around about it then, but believe me, it's camouflaged behind a partition that's against the wall behind her desk. Trust me, it's there!"

Danielle entered the dressing room, carrying a floor-length veil over her arm. Placing it on my head, she smiled. "Now that complements and completes your gown so well. I chose this because I know that the color teal has a special significance for you and Claudia."

As she spread the floor-length veil behind me, tears began streaming from my eyes. The edges of the entire veil were embroidered in a delicate, teal floral design.

Claudia reached over and handed me a tissue. "I think you're right, Al. No need to try on anything else. That's the one!"

Turning to Danielle, I pulled myself together and handed her an envelope with five one-hundred-dollar bills in it. "I am sure this is the one. Here is my deposit for the dress and veil. Claudia can help me get out of this gown. Could we just have a few minutes, so I can finish composing myself?"

"Absolutely! Take your time. When you're ready, come out into the front of the shop, and I'll have your receipt ready for you."

As soon as Danielle stepped out of the dressing room, Claudia turned to me. "Okay, let's get you out of this gown!"

We carefully hung the dress back on its hanger and placed it on a hook in the dressing room. As I finished getting dressed, Claudia carefully slid the desk and partition in the corner of the room, just far enough away from the wall for us to get the door open. As we gathered our things, I looked back at the gown hanging on the wall. "That dress is so beautiful. I hope I make it back safely to wear it!"

Whirling around, Claudia scoffed. "What kind of crazy talk is that? Knock it off, Allie. Of course, you'll be back!"

Hesitating, I reached into my bag, pulled out an envelope, and whispered, "Wait, Claudia, I wrote a note for Danielle. Just let me leave it here with the dress."

As I hooked Brick's leash back on his harness, he immediately got up and moved with Claudia and me as we slipped out.

Racing out the door and around the corner, we grabbed a cab and headed to Portsmouth to get Claudia's father's car. To make it more challenging to trace us, we had the driver drop us off about ten blocks from the storage garage and walked the rest of the way.

Chapter 16

Fifteen minutes later, Danielle turned to Antonio. "I wonder if the girls are almost ready. I'll go check on them."

Standing in the dressing room entrance, she called out, "Claudia, are you both about ready?"

There was only silence. Stepping just inside the threshold, she stopped dead in her tracks and gazed around the room. "Allie? Claudia? Where are you?"

She spotted Allie's gown hanging neatly on the wall with a note tucked into the neckline. Instinctively, she turned toward her desk and noticed they had pulled it from the wall.

Moving back over to grab the note left with the dress, she rushed out to Antonio. "I don't know what to tell you, sir."

He jumped from his chair as if someone had hit an ejector button. "What?"

"Allie and Claudia have left."

"How could they? They never came through the shop!"

Motioning to follow her, she led him back to the dressing room. Audibly sighing, she pointed toward her desk in the corner. "There is a back entrance to the building. I usually have that partition and my desk up against the wall to block it off, but—"

"But one of them knew it was there! Crap!"

"Wait, they left me this note."

As she opened up the envelope, she began reading.

Danielle,

Thank you so much for fitting us into your schedule at the last minute today. I can't wait to wear my new wedding gown down the aisle to marry the love of my life. I know there will be a final fitting as the day gets closer. I will be in touch.

Thank you again,

Allie Callahan.

Looking up from the note, she stuttered, "I'm sure they must be close by."

"Thank you, ah…it's Danielle, right?"

"Yes, I'm sure you're right!"

Before he even completed his thought, Antonio spun on his heels and moved to the door behind the desk. "If you don't mind, I think I'll use this exit and see if I can catch up with them." Without waiting for an answer, he hurried out the door.

Jogging out and around the building, he stopped on the sidewalk, looking in all directions. There was no sign of Allie or Claudia, and they had at least a fifteen- to twenty-minute start on him. His mind was racing. *Why in the hell would they just take off?* What was even worse, how was he ever going to explain this to Payne?

Moving down the sidewalk to his car, he ripped his cell phone from his pocket and dialed Payne's cell number. It went directly to voice mail. He tried his office phone, but it went to voice mail, too, after four rings. Speaking out loud to himself, he growled. "Shit, Payne, where the eff are you?"

Sliding into his car, he called the station directly. Stacy Anderson answered. "Stanford Police Department, how can I help you?"

"Stacy, it's Antonio. I'm trying to reach Payne. Is he at the station?"

"Yes, he's in the war room having a meeting right now."

"Please get him on the phone. It's urgent!"

In ten seconds, she had him on the phone. "Payne here!"

"Payne, this is Antonio. Am I on speaker?"

"Yes."

"Please call me back on my cell, sir?"

Standing, Payne excused himself, but Josh stopped him. "Hey, Payne, what's going on? Isn't Antonio with Allie and Claudia?"

Thinking it was probably nothing, Jake jumped in. "Give him a minute, Josh. He'll be right back."

"Right, just give me a couple of minutes."

As he left the conference room and headed to his office, Payne pulled out his cell phone and made the call. Antonio answered on the first ring.

"Antonio, what the hell is going on?"

"There is no easy way to put this Payne. Allie and Claudia have slipped away from me!"

"What?"

After a long pause, Antonio blurted out, "Payne? Are you there?"

"What the hell happened, Antonio?"

"I don't rightly know, sir. I took them to a bridal shop for an appointment they had made yesterday. Everything was going fine. Nothing seemed out of the ordinary. After they were done trying on dresses, I was waiting for them to come out into the shop so we could leave. When they still hadn't come out of the dressing room fifteen minutes later, the shop owner, Danielle, went back to check on them, and they were gone."

"Gone? Gone how? How did they ever get out without you seeing them?"

"There is a door that leads to a back entrance. It's usually blocked by a partition and the owner's desk, but apparently, Claudia knew about it. They used that exit and must have had at least a fifteen- to-twenty-minute lead on me."

"You drove them there, right?"

"Yes, sir, I did."

"Well, that means they must be on foot or using some type of public transportation then, right?"

"Yes, and they have the dog. Traveling on buses and trains is difficult with a dog. Maybe a taxi or Uber is their only choice."

"Okay, Antonio, I am going to put out an APB and check to see if they have used a taxi or Uber. Unless there was a cab on the street, they would need to use a credit card to secure one. You keep combing the area in your vehicle and see if you can spot them."

The words no sooner left his mouth when Josh and Jake walked into his office.

Growing more concerned, Jake asked, "Spot who?"

"Jake, Josh, please come in and have a seat. We need to talk!"

Chapter 17

There was still no news about Claudia's and Allie's whereabouts at seven o'clock. Josh and Jake were in the war room, pacing the floor when Antonio walked in with Payne.

Rushing over, Josh stopped directly in front of them. "Any word?"

Antonio looked to the floor and then directly up into Josh's eyes. "No, buddy, sorry! Nothing yet!"

Looking to Payne and then to Jake for reassurance, Josh pleaded, "But no news, in this case, is good news, right? I mean, we think they left on their own accord."

"That is true, but what concerns us is that they have no protection. Do either of you know why they might have decided to leave now? Have they said anything out of the ordinary to either of you?"

Josh interjected. "Jake, how about last night when they made that joke about escaping today?"

"Damn, you're right. They were kind of talking in circles, but honestly, they're always kidding around and saying the craziest things. It's hard to know when they are joking or really trying to cover their tracks."

Payne closed his eyes as he ran his hands through his hair in frustration. "Okay, what exactly did they say?"

"Over dinner, Claudia made a joke about their trip to the bridal shop the next day. Honestly, I just thought they were trying to keep us from wanting to join them."

Payne pressed again. "Just exactly what did Claudia say, Jake?"

Rubbing his hands together, he brought them to his forehead and closed his eyes in frustration. "I didn't think much about it at the time..." Looking back up at Payne, he recollected, "She said something like, 'Hey, Allie, should we tell them about our secret plans to run away?'"

Josh spun around. "Payne, they were just joking around! How could we have known?"

"You couldn't. I guess that's the point. Maybe it was their way of letting you know after the fact that they were planning it all along. Look, I think it is time to call it a day here. Antonio, why don't you escort Josh and Jake home. I am putting a team on this tonight. If we hear anything at all, we'll call you."

Antonio, Josh, and Jake were back at the apartment by eight o'clock. As they entered the foyer, Jake turned. "Anyone up to eating something? I'm not really hungry, but we need to keep our strength up, just in case they need us for something."

Antonio agreed. "Yeah, you guys should eat and at least try to get some rest."

Josh grunted, following Jake to the kitchen. "What the hell were they thinking?"

Clearing his throat, Jake scoffed. "Clearly, they weren't! At least not as far as I'm concerned, they weren't!"

When Jake reached the refrigerator, he yelled out, "Hey, Antonio, Josh, come here quick!"

As Antonio entered the doorway, Jake was holding up two envelopes. "Looks like they didn't leave without letting us know something!"

Chapter 18

During the first few hours of the trip, we hardly spoke. Finally, I saw the sign Welcome to Connecticut. Breaking the silence, I turned to Claudia. "I sure hope we're doing the right thing. I mean, leaving without telling anyone where we're going."

"Are you kidding? You're questioning that now? Look, we didn't have a choice. They never would have let us out of their sight, not even for a minute. Even grandfather said we had to stop Makya! Just us alone, no one else."

"In my heart, I know you're right, but—"

"Look, Allie, I've given it some thought. If we travel at night and sleep during the day, we will be less likely spotted. Don't you agree?"

"I think you're absolutely right, but I think I will need to stretch my legs soon."

Claudia drove a few more miles and then pulled into a 7-Eleven. While she filled the gas tank, I walked Brick and used the restroom. When we were both back in the car, Claudia handed me a coffee. "I think we need some caffeine if we are going to stay awake and not stop until morning."

Sticking to our plan, we drove another eight hours and then pulled off the road at a small hotel in Ohio. That day, we slept as much as we could. Before we got on the road again, late that afternoon, we listened to the national news to see if we had made the headlines. There was nothing; it was radio silence.

We grabbed something to eat before we headed out again. There was a small diner next door, so we went over to eat. We parked right next to the building so we could keep an eye on Brick in the SUV from the diner window. "We'll be right back, boy. You watch the car."

As we entered the diner, a waitress from behind the counter called out, "Have a seat, ladies. I'll be right with you."

Claudia huffed. "I just want to know when we graduated from girls to ladies. That drives me bonkers!"

"Look at her, Claudia. She can't be more than sixteen. To her, we probably look like middle-aged women."

Picking up the menu on the table, Claudia sneered. "Hey! Just how old do you think we look, anyway?"

The young waitress approached our table with a pot of coffee. She looked first in Claudia's direction. "Coffee, ma'am?"

Lifting only her eyes from the menu, Claudia's expression was priceless. I couldn't hold it back and I burst out laughing.

Confused by my reaction, the young woman stepped back. "I'm sorry. Did I say something wrong?"

Looking up, I tried to compose myself. "No, it's okay. We just didn't get much sleep last night, and we're a bit giddy and maybe one of us is just a little too sensitive. Could we just have a few minutes to look over the menu?"

"Of course! My name is Janis. When you're ready to order, just let me know!"

As Janis walked away from our table, Claudia looked up from her menu. A big grin came across her face as she stood and excused herself. "I know, I know, I'm the sensitive one. I don't know why you think it's so funny when people call us ladies or ma'am. I have to use the restroom. When Janis comes back, just order me some bacon, eggs, and toast."

"No home fries?"

"No, thank you, no home fries!"

After Claudia left the table, a young girl walked up and sat across from me in the booth. She didn't speak, but just sat there, looking at me, tilting her head back and forth in a questioning manner.

When I reached across the table, she jolted back, as if she thought I might strike her. Withdrawing my arm, I asked, "Are you all right?"

"Am I all right? Am I all right? Of course, I'm not all right! Do I look all right to you?"

"You look a bit tired to me, but except for that, you look fine!"

The waitress walked up to the table. "I heard you speaking. Were you trying to get my attention?"

The young girl on the other side of the table spoke up. "You better answer her. She can't see me."

"Why, yes, I just wanted to order some bacon, eggs, and toast for me and my friend, Claudia."

"No hash browns or home fries?"

"No, thank you."

Looking back across the table, the young girl was gone, but Claudia was back and climbing into the booth. "Did you order?"

"Yes, bacon, eggs and toast, no home fries."

Chapter 19

That same morning, Antonio followed Josh and Jake to the station. Jake's cell phone rang as they climbed the stairs to the front entrance. It was Payne. Stopping short to answer, Jake grabbed Josh's arm and gestured for him to wait.

"Good morning, Payne."

There was a long pause as he rolled his eyes and nodded. "Yes, we just arrived." After another long silence, he sighed. "Yes, we have them, and we'll come right up to your office." Hanging up, he reached for one of the doors and opened it for Josh. "Well, I guess I don't have to tell you who that was."

"No, you certainly don't!"

"He wants to see the notes that the girls left us for all the good they might do. They really don't say much at all."

As Josh and Jake arrived at Payne's office, Antonio was right on their heels.

Standing, Payne didn't even give them a chance to sit down. "Don't get comfortable, guys. We're going down to the war room. I believe we're going to need as much help as we can get to figure out where our two amateur sleuths have gone. We have a lot of work to do, and to help with that, I have called in the entire team! I'm sure they took some sort of amazing tools from Allie's ancestral box, and, of course, there are Allie's incredible gifts, but she has somehow got it in her head that she has to do this on her own. Did you bring in the notes that Claudia and Allie left for you?"

"Yes, Payne, but they are really short and to the point. Nothing to give us any clues. They basically both apologized in their notes, told us how much they love us, and said that they would be back as soon as they could. That's all!

Chapter 20

Two days later, we made it to the Ozarks. As we drove up and around the lake, Claudia was awe-struck.

"This is so beautiful, Allie. If your family has had a cabin up here all these years, why have we never visited it?"

"To be honest, it was so far away, coming here never really occurred to me." I pointed ahead. "There should be a small wooden church just up around the next curve in the road. It sits back a little in the woods on the right. Right there, there it is!"

As Claudia pulled into the circular drive and stopped in front of the chapel, she put the SUV in park and gazed at the building. "Allie, what a quaint little church! I wonder how old it is."

"It's really old, and it's just the same as I remember it. It is still in great shape. Someone has really maintained it all these years."

"Wait, as you remember it? Do you mean from when you were a small child?"

"No, from a different time or dimension, when I married Josh. Well, a version of Josh. His name was James then."

"Al, we need to try to put some kind of timeline together so I can keep all these versions of us straight! I can't keep up with them all in my head."

"I know. Look, Claudia, we need to take Brick out for a short walk. It's been a few hours. Do you think you could do that while I go in and see if anyone is here?"

"Sure thing!"

Stepping up to the entrance of the chapel, I tried the door. It was unlocked. Opening it, I stepped into the vestibule of the church. Standing at the chapel's back entrance took me aback. It was much smaller than I remembered. Moving into the chapel, I made my way down to the altar and stopped. Closing my eyes, the memories came flooding back. James's face and expression were as clear in my mind's eye as the day I married him circa 1920.

A voice rang out behind me. "You need to go. Get out of here! Right now!" I turned to find the young girl from the diner standing in the aisle of the chapel. Tears were streaming down her face.

Moving toward her, I pleaded, "How can I help you? Why are you here?"

Backing away from me, she appeared unsettled. "Please, I am begging you! Get out of here right now. You are in great danger. If you don't leave, you will never make it back in time to help me!"

As she vanished into thin air, Brick was growling outside. Panic welled up inside me as I sprinted to the back of the church, just as Claudia came into the vestibule with Brick, who was frantically barking.

"Claudia, get out, get out now!" When she didn't move, I yelled, "Claudia, we have to get out of here!"

Using my body to force her out the door, she tripped, sending us both tumbling down the front stairs with Brick at our heels. Suddenly, the heat of a massive explosion blew out above us, and the entire sky lit up. My ears rang as I pushed myself up on my knees and aided Claudia to her feet. Once on her feet, she pulled me up, grabbed Brick's leash, and we bolted toward the SUV.

Adrenalin coursed through my veins as I loaded Brick into the car, and we both leaped in. "Drive, Claudia, get moving! Take a right at the end of the driveway."

My ears were still ringing as Claudia pulled out on the road. Turning to me, she began yelling, "Allie, what the hell is going on? Was that meant for us, or just some crazy coincidence?"

"Claudia, just keep driving. The cabin is just a short distance from here. I hope it is still intact!"

"Oh ,my God, Al, that was so close!"

"I know, I know! Keep driving. If I remember correctly, a private road right up here on the left leads to our cabin."

"Allie, are you kidding? What do you mean, if you remember? OMG!"

"There, there it is! Take that left. See the sign: Private Keep Out? That's it."

"I hope you're right, because Private Keep Out means just that. I don't want anyone to come out of a cabin with shotguns blazing to chase us off!"

"No, Claudia, it's okay, this is it! I'm sure I recognize this."

Once we got far enough down the dirt road and out of eyeshot of the main road, Claudia pulled over and put the SUV in park. "Alrighty then, let's take a deep breath."

A voice from the back seat chimed in. "I think that's a splendid idea. We should all take a deep breath and just stop and collect our thoughts."

I turned, looking toward the backseat. "I don't think anyone asked you!"

Claudia opened the door and stepped out of the car. "Unless your name is Dr. Doolittle, and you're talking to Brick, I will assume we are no longer alone!"

I grimaced. "Yes, you are correct!"

"Yes, you can now communicate with animals, or yes, we have a ghostly guest in tow now?"

"Ah, yes, we have a guest with us now."

"And may I ask their name?"

"You can ask, but I don't know that yet!"

"And how long have we had this guest with us?"

Once again, my twisted face gave me away. "I think since the diner?"

"OMG, Allie, you need to tell me these things. We have no privacy when this happens!"

The voice in the back seat rang out again. "Okay, my name is Emily, and you might want to tell your friend, Claudia, that I just saved both of your lives!"

"Claudia, get back in the car. I think you will be glad she is here with us, and besides, she just told me her name is Emily."

"Emily? Is that all she has to say for herself?"

"Ah, no! I think there is one more crucial fact you should know."

"Oh, and what might that be?"

"She just saved our lives in that church back there. She's the one who warned me and got us out of there in time."

"Stepping up into the SUV, Claudia grunted. "Yes, that is crucial information to know. If you're still with us, thank you, Emily."

Chapter 21

Sure enough, we drove just a short distance more and came upon the cabin. Opening the door, I climbed out of the SUV.

"Wow, it has barely changed. Look, the shrubs need a little trimming, but, all in all, it doesn't look that bad." I turned around to face Claudia. "I guess a log cabin doesn't really change much over the years."

I let Brick out of the car, and he followed us up the porch steps to the front door. Emily spoke up. "Maybe we should knock?"

"No, no one has lived here for a long time."

Claudia rolled her eyes. "We still have company, don't we?"

"Yes, we do. I'll try to be better at interpreting and improve communications for you both."

Bending down, I lifted the mat. "There must be a key here somewhere? Well, I guess that's not the hiding place. Maybe there is a planter or something around with a key."

Claudia sat on one of the porch chairs. "Are you telling me we came all this way and you didn't check with your mom for a key?"

"Well, I couldn't really do that, could I? If I asked her for a key, she would know where we went."

"Yeah, you do have a point there. Wait, Allie, look up. Above the door jamb. Is that a key poking out?"

Jumping up, I knocked it down. "It sure is!"

"Great, we're in!"

Unlocking the door, I pushed it open. As it swung in, it took a wall of cobwebs with it, clearing the threshold from what resembled *Charlotte's Web*. "Well, it looks like the inside needs a little more attention than the outside does."

Covering her mouth with her sleeve, Claudia walked in the door. "Crap, it's more than a little dusty in here. I think there might be almost as much dirt on this floor as there is in the yard outside. Just look at this place; it looks like we're walking into a time warp. It doesn't look like anyone has updated this place for a hundred years!"

Stepping in and gazing around the room, I chuckled. "You're damn close. As a matter of fact, everything is exactly how I remember it the last time I laid eyes on it. I remember it so clearly, just like it was yesterday. See that brass bed over in the corner? James and I christened it the night before our wedding. I can still almost feel the sensation of the heat and humidity dripping from our skin as we made love into the wee hours of the morning. And look over there next to the bed. That's the washstand and basin we bathed ourselves in that morning before our wedding."

Moving across the room, I stopped and, running my hand over a beautiful folding partition made of fabric, I sighed. "And Claudia, see this? James stood behind it when he got dressed on our wedding day. I'll never forget how he looked when he stepped out from behind it in that pinstriped suit.

He was the most handsome and debonair man I had ever seen!"

"Ah, Earth to Allie! This is your friend, Claudia, speaking! Please come down out of the clouds!"

"I know, I know, but I just can't help it. I'm not sure who I miss more, James or Josh!"

Taking me by the shoulders, Claudia spun me to face her. "Ugh! Allie, aren't they the same person? Well, so to speak?"

"Of course, they are, but I had you going for a minute! Didn't I? Sorry, Claudia, I was just caught up in the moment!"

"Well, Al, we need to stay in the present, because we have a lot of cleaning to do. If you think I'll be sleeping in here for even one night without disinfecting this place, you really don't know me very well!"

"You're right! We definitely need some food and supplies, starting with a good disinfectant! Let's get in the SUV and go back to that general store we passed on our way here. What was the name of it? First Dawn General Store?"

"But, Allie, that is back quite a way, isn't it? Wasn't it on Main Street near Route 72?"

"It sure was, but it's just far enough from here to keep us off the radar if someone gets lucky enough to get that close to finding us. And look, if anyone is curious and asks where we're staying, we can just say we are camping down the road apiece."

"I certainly hope you're right! I'm starved and really too hungry to debate you on the subject! Surely Brick could use something to eat as well."

As soon as Claudia said his name, he was on his feet and headed to the door. "Okay, boy, let's go get some food!"

Chapter 22

As we headed out to the general store, I pulled a folded sheet of paper from my pocket, handing it to Claudia. "Here's a list of things we need to purchase."

Taking it out of my hand and unfolding it, Claudia snickered. "What? When did you write this list? I didn't know anything about it."

"Look, we need to be prepared for anything. I wrote it yesterday in the hotel before you woke up. Do you know how bad it will be if we end up having to track Makya through this terrain?"

"Well, from the looks of this list, I apparently have no idea!" She began reading. "Let me see, a first-aid kit, hiking backpacks, hiking boots, a map, sleeping bags, bug repellent, bug repellent clothing. Are you kidding me? Do they actually sell bug repellent clothing?"

"Yes, they do. Let's hope they carry them in this little store!"

Claudia read on. "Two jackknives, extra food, extra water, energy bars, sunscreen, extra socks, and hats, and four burner phones. Looks like you forgot a compass!"

"Nope, look in the glove compartment. It's in there with two headlamps, extra batteries, and a zip-lock bag with several boxes of wooden matches."

"Holy shit, Allie! Damn, you really are serious about this hiking crap, aren't you?"

"You don't really think Makya is going to come to us willingly, do you? I am sure he will try to lure us out of the cabin and confront us in the worst place possible. Anyway, I just want us to be prepared. What's not on that list are cleaning supplies, a cooler and ice for our food at the cabin, as well as some clean sheets for that bed."

When we arrived at the store, I turned to Claudia. "We need to keep our eyes and ears open and our mouths shut!"

"And what is that supposed to mean?"

"Remember what grandfather used to say? We have two ears, two eyes, and only one mouth for a reason!"

"Very funny!"

"Look, the less we talk, the less likely we are to say the wrong thing. And besides, we certainly don't want the store clerks to remember the two lovely young women who came in to buy a bunch of camping supplies! We don't want this to be a memorable selling experience for whoever waits on us."

"Okay, I get it!"

Getting out of the car, I moved over to Claudia. "I think we should divide and conquer. I'll gather up the camping supplies on this list and the burner phones. You get us the cleaning supplies, cooler, ice, food, and sheets for the bed. Oh yes, and a forty-pound bag of dog food for Brick."

As we stepped into the store, I turned to Claudia. "Ugh, I don't think this is the kind of General Store I was expecting."

A woman stepped into the aisle in front of us. "Good afternoon, my name is Dawn. Can I help you with something?"

"Hello, Dawn. This is a beautiful store, but not at all what we expected. We thought this was a small general store where we could buy things we needed in the way of groceries and camping supplies."

"Well, it used to be. In fact, this little general store used to be the closest thing to a big box store this little town had. They sold everything from candy and groceries to nails and plumbing supplies. Unfortunately, this store just couldn't compete with those big box stores and became obsolete. I like to think that because the store still stands here and we offer vintage and antique items, we're keeping those times alive in people's memories.

Claudia just couldn't help herself as she stepped up to a counter in the middle of the store. "That is so inspiring, and what a noble thing to do for your town."

"Why, thank you! What did you say your name was?"

As she opened her mouth to speak, Claudia looked in my direction as I shot her a dagger!

"Ah, I didn't. My name is Celeste. Yes, Celeste Forest."

I reached up to rub my forehead in an attempt to rub away a headache I could feel coming on. "Could you tell us where we might find a general store that might have the things we are looking for all in one place?"

"I'm sorry to say that our little town has lost that kind of shopping experience with the influx of the big box stores. You could probably find most of what you need at Walmart. There's also Dick's Sporting Goods, and if all else fails, there is always the Dollar General."

"Well, thank you so much, Dawn. We'll check those places for what we need." Tapping on Claudia's shoulder, I began backing out of the store.

"You're very welcome! If you're ever in need of antiques, please stop back by."

As we stepped out of the store, I grabbed Claudia by the arm. "Celeste Forest? Are you kidding me? Celest Forest?"

Before she could respond, we heard Brick barking and growling at someone in an old Chevy pickup, spinning his tires and speeding out of the parking lot.

A teenage girl stepped over to us. "Oh, don't pay any attention to him. He's just showing out! Nobody around here pays any attention to him."

I glanced over to Claudia. I could see that she wanted to say something, but she kept quiet!

As I stepped up into the SUV, I smiled. "Why, thank you, miss!"

"You're welcome, ma'am! My name's Dolly."

Rolling down the window, I smiled again. "Well then, thank you, Dolly."

As I pulled out of the parking lot, Claudia couldn't hold it in any longer. "Well, wasn't that the strangest thing?"

A sad, whimpering voice in the back seat whispered, "That's my cousin. She's in desperate need of some help, but I can't be the one to do the helping, as you well know. She can't even see me."

Looking in the rearview mirror, I responded, "Is that why you have been attached to us since the diner?"

Claudia turned to look in the back seat. "Let me guess! Emily again?"

"Yes, it sure is! Apparently, Dolly is Emily's cousin. Emily is so sad. She just said that Dolly is in serious need of help, but she can't help her."

95

"Well, of course, she can't help her. Dolly can't even see her!"

"You know we are going to have to figure out a way to help her, right?"

Emily cried out, "Really? You will help her? You are both so kind!"

Chapter 23

We decided on Walmart, which was a great choice. We purchased everything on our list, except the bug repellent clothing.

When we finally made it back to the cabin, we were famished. We fed Brick first, made ourselves some sandwiches, and had a picnic on the porch.

After eating, we cleaned and finished just as the sun started setting. It was perfect timing because the tree covering over the cabin darkened the rooms early, forcing us to use candles and the two Coleman lanterns.

After lighting the lanterns and placing them around the room, I grabbed the large pitcher from the washbasin and a flashlight.

"Claudia, I'm taking Brick. I'll be right back."

"Where are you going?"

"To get some water."

"Water? Where?"

"Just outside, a little way from here. At the spring."

"Wait, I'm coming!"

"No, I'll be fine. I will be within earshot."

I returned a few minutes later with the pitcher filled to the brim with water.

As I carefully filled the washbasin with half the water, I joked, "I think all the dirt we cleaned out of this cabin now covers our bodies. We can't get in those clean sheets like this. Do you want to clean up first, or should I?"

Claudia didn't respond.

"Well?"

She finally broke the silence. "You expect us to clean with the small amount of water in that basin? Why can't we go down to the spring and take a dip?"

"Well, that is an option, but we will probably get eaten alive in the time that it takes us to get down to the spring, wash up, and get back here. The mosquitoes are so big out there you could put saddles on them."

"Well then, I guess I'll go first!"

After she got washed up, I opened the window and dumped the dirty water outside on the ground.

Looking rather disgusted, Claudia remarked, "It looks like you've done this before!"

"You could say that!"

Finally, at nine o'clock, we turned in. It had been a long few days for us, and we were both exhausted. Setting a lantern on the nightstand next to me, we pulled down the sheets and climbed into bed.

Claudia pulled herself up, leaning on one elbow to face me, letting out an audible sigh. "I wonder how Josh and Jake are doing? I mean, they are probably worried sick!"

"I'm sure they are, but I'm trying not to think about it. I'm sure they're both pretty damn angry with us as well! We can't worry about that now. We have to stay focused! Keep our eye on the goal, so to speak."

"The goal being Makya, right?

"Right! But for now, our focus should be on sleep, so let's get some."

Turning over, I turned off the Colman lantern and closed my eyes.

It wasn't even a minute later when Claudia's voice broke through the silence. "Hey, Al, are we really just going to ignore what happened at the church today? We haven't even talked about it!"

Shifting in the bed, I rolled over to face her. "I know. It's so strange. It seems so surreal to me. I mean, because we didn't get hurt, and it happened so fast it almost feels—"

"I know. It almost feels like it didn't happen at all. It's weird, isn't it?"

Emily's voice chimed in from the other side of the room. "Oh, it happened all right! Some dude was there in the church about an hour before you guys and rigged the whole thing up!"

"And you're just telling me this now?" I shot up, climbed out of bed, and turned the lantern back on.

Emily was standing on the other side of the room, just in front of the cabin entrance.

Sitting up in bed, Claudia rolled her eyes in frustration. "This would be a good time to help Emily and I communicate better! Like, what did she just tell you? What the heck is going on?"

"Emily just said that she saw a man at the church about an hour before we got there setting up the explosion."

"Allie, that doesn't mean it was meant for us or even that it was Makya who did it. Couldn't it still be a mere coincidence? I mean, how could Makya or anyone else know we would be there at that moment and then just blow up the church?"

Turning back to Emily, I asked, "Okay, so can you describe the guy you saw at the church?"

"Well, I couldn't really see what he looked like because he had on a hoodie, and it was closed tightly around his face, but he was a big guy! I sure wouldn't want to meet him in a dark alley at night!"

"Come on, Claudia, this had to be Makya. Like me, he has the ability to know and do things that others can't. Come on, you know that! Are you kidding? I know it's a stretch, but he may have foreseen that we would be there.

"And something else that I think is really odd is that no matter where we went today, not one person was talking about the explosion at the church. Don't you think that's strange?"

"To be honest, we didn't stay anywhere long enough to hear many conversations, so no, I don't think that's strange. I think it's probably odder that the two of us haven't discussed it until now. Especially since we could have been killed.

I don't know, Al. We have been so focused on making a safe place for us to stay; I kind of understand that. One thing is for sure, I think we should pick up a newspaper tomorrow and see what it says about the explosion."

Chapter 24

Bright and early the following day, the horrible odor of hot breath swept across my face, waking me in the worst possible way. I opened my eyes to find Brick resting his head on the bed so close that our noses were almost touching. Pushing him away, I gagged. "Oh, Brick, you have terrible morning breath! You're a great dog, but you need a toothbrush. Yuck!"

Claudia laughed, waving her hand in front of her face. "Yeah, that was my wake-up call this morning as well. I agree we get that boy a toothbrush ASAP, and as soon as you get him home, take him to the vet for a good teeth cleaning. Pew!"

"That's a great idea! No argument there!"

Getting up, I dragged myself across the cabin and sat at the table where Claudia so graciously handed me a mug of coffee. "Thank you so much. I need a kick-start this morning!"

"I know you haven't had time to have your coffee yet, Allie, but what's on our agenda today? I was thinking about my pendent. What grandfather told us seems so obvious to me. A string named C has to be an old piano string, don't you think? The only problem is, where is the piano?"

Tucking my hair behind my ears, I leaned back in my chair. "That would seem the logical conclusion, but at the same time, maybe a little too obvious. First, to my knowledge, there was never a piano here at the cabin.

Pausing to think, I took another sip of coffee. "But you know what? Years ago, that little chapel that blew up used to have an old player piano in its small reception hall and an old organ in the chapel. To be honest, the organ there years ago was very small. The one I saw in there before the explosion was much larger, with very tall pipes. I'm sure it was much newer."

"Wait, Allie, that would make more sense. Maybe Makya's target wasn't us after all. It was probably to destroy the piano or organ that my pendant was hidden in."

"You're right! Well, if that's the case, we are out of luck. They are both surely burned and melted down to mere ashes and scrap metal now."

"Nope, you guys are wrong about that! Well, at least about the organ."

"Claudia, Emily just popped in. She says we're wrong about the organ."

Taking a sip of her coffee, Claudia scanned the room as if Emily would suddenly appear to her. "Okay, Emily, spill it!"

"If that's where the pendent is, it may still be safe and sound. Miss Dawn, the New Dawn General Store owner, purchased the organ. Well, not from the church, but when she bought the store, they held an auction, and she purchased it then. The previous owner had it on the store's second floor for years. It is still sitting on the right-hand side of the first floor of her store, even as we speak."

Pouring myself a second cup of coffee, I turned to Claudia. "Well, long story short, it looks like we will be paying a visit to the First Dawn General Store today, right after breakfast. Apparently, the original organ from the church may be there."

Claudia perked right up. "Alrighty then, shopping at the vintage general store it is."

"No, Claudia, I know how much you love antiques and vintage items, but that is not on our agenda today! We are on a necklace-finding mission only! Got it?"

"Yeah, but Al, you truly can be a buzzkill sometimes, you know. I mean, what would it hurt to just look around?"

"Claudia?"

Emily piped in. "I have to agree with her. You are a Debbie downer!"

"No one asked you, Emily."

Claudia burst out laughing. "She agreed with me, didn't she?"

Chapter 25

By ten o'clock, we were back at the general store. When we walked in, the owner, Miss Dawn, was helping other customers. Waving, she called across the store, "Hello, ladies. So glad you're back! I'll be right with you."

Claudia smirked and leaned into me. "Well, so much for remaining unmemorable. I suspect that moment has passed."

Taking Claudia by the arm, I whispered, "Don't make a big deal about this."

Pulling her to the right-hand side of the store, I stopped short and stood in amazement. There it was, sitting right there in all its glory, just as Emily had told us. I moved closer and sat down in front of the organ. Gently running my fingers over the keyboard, I sighed. "It's in amazing condition. It must be well over a hundred years old."

Running her hand over its wood finish, Claudia let out an audible breath. "Geeze, Al, it's so beautiful! Do you think this is the one you remember?"

A voice rang out behind us. "Do you play?"

Turning around, Miss Dawn was standing there, sweetly, smiling back at me.

"Ah, yes, but I couldn't!"

"Of course, you can! That's what it's made for. An instrument is meant to be played. It may not sound like it did when it was brand new, but please, by all means, give her a try."

Positioning my hands carefully on the keys, I hesitated. "I'll try, but trust me, it's been a while! I began playing a song my grandmother taught me when I was just a small child, and when I was done, I went right into a verse of "Amazing Grace."

Placing her hand on my shoulder, Claudia asked, "What was the first tune you played? It sounded so familiar."

"It was that little song Grandmother used to sing to us. Don't you remember? Santos, which she told us means Holy."

"Oh, yeah! I remember that!"

Miss Dawn stepped over to the side of the organ. "Well, that was beautiful!"

Standing from the bench, I paused to choose my words carefully. "We actually have a favor to ask."

"What is it?"

As I lifted the key and the pendent from my neck to explain, she interrupted me. "Well, what do you know! That looks like the type of key that might belong to this organ."

Stunned, I shook my head. "You're kidding, right?"

"No! Not in the least. The key to this old organ has been missing for years. This old instrument has quite a history, or so I've been told. I understand that the previous store owner's family purchased it and brought it here for sentimental reasons, or at least that's how the story goes. It was such a shame. It just sat upstairs, out of sight, collecting dust until I bought it at auction before they sold this store."

"Really? Do you know where the previous owners purchased it?"

"I was told they purchased it from that little chapel in the woods. You must have heard about that little church that burned down yesterday?"

Tipping my head in a questioning manner, my eyebrows raised, I grimaced. "Well, do you mind if I just try this key and see if it works?"

"No, by all means! Give it a try."

Rolling my eyes in Claudia's direction, I carefully slid the key into the keyhole and took a deep breath. "Here goes!"

As I turned the key, there was a slight clicking and then a release. We were in! Hanging just inside the opening was a braided necklace designed with delicate pieces of animal skin. Woven into one end was a small stone with the letter C carved into it. At the other end, resting on the inside of the bottom of the open space, was the missing pendant.

Claudia stepped back and began babbling. "That's it! A string named C. That's what Grandfather was talking about! It's just as Grandfather described it. OMG, it's just beautiful!"

Miss Dawn reached in and pulled out the necklace and turned toward me. "This pendant looks a lot like yours."

"Yes, it's a long story, but these pendants have been passed down in our families for generations. This pendant belonged to Claudia's family and should have been passed down to her. Years ago, it was stolen and somehow ended up in this organ. We would be happy to purchase it from you if you would be willing to sell it to us?"

"Don't be ridiculous. A piece like this is priceless!"

As I turned toward Claudia, I could see the color slowly draining from her face. Turning back to Miss Dawn, I pleaded. "Please, name your price. You have no idea how important this piece is to us both!"

"There is no price. It belongs to you."

Stepping forward, she slipped it over Claudia's neck and smiled. "What do you say? You give me the key, and we'll call it even." Stepping back to admire the pendent, she winked. "After all, that pendant really belongs to your friend here."

"Thank you so much! You have no idea how much this means to us!"

Miss Dawn chuckled. "Oh, I think you might be surprised by what I know! Huh, Emily?"

Emily stepped out from behind Claudia. "Uh-huh!"

As another customer came into the store, she turned from us. "Don't worry girls, your secrets are safe with me. If anyone comes calling, I never saw you!"

Chapter 26

By eleven-thirty, we were back at the cabin. As we stepped in the door, Claudia started on me right away!

"Hey, Allie, what do you say we try a little traveling? Like a practice session before lunch? I do have my pendant now. Can we at least try it out?"

Giving no credence to her request, I turned, moved over to the counter, and opened the cooler. "I don't think I can do anything on an empty stomach, much less travel between time or any other dimension. Aren't you even a little hungry? What do you say to a ham and cheese sandwich?"

And there it was, that sweet, pleading face I could never resist. "Come on, Allie. What do you say? Just a small little short practice travel? Just for a few minutes!"

My face twisted into that look I always got just before I gave in to her, and with hesitation in my voice, I squeaked out, "I don't know, Claudia. Why don't we have lunch and do a little planning first?"

Oh, come on, Allie, please!

"You're impossible, Claudia. I've never traveled with anyone else before. I don't even know what to expect."

"You almost did. Well, before you stopped me the other night. Please!"

"I don't know how you talk me into these things. Okay, just a short little trip, that's it. Then back here for lunch!"

Closing the cooler, I paused for thought. Moving across the room, I sat down on the floor in front of the fireplace. "Claudia, come over and sit here in front of me. We'll hold hands like we did the other night and see what happens."

After a few seconds, a frustrated Claudia squinted in frustration. "Nothing, absolutely nothing!"

"Look, you have to be a little more patient than that! Think back. What were you thinking about the other night when you almost time traveled?"

"I was really tired and kind of during out! Like, just daydreaming about when we were kids."

"Okay, why don't you try to think of a fun place where we spent time together when we were younger? Just kind of daze out and think of that place and time. Let's see what happens."

After a minute, I could feel that strange sensation I always got when I was slipping away. Soon we were both sitting in low lounge chairs on the beach at my beach house in Maine. I could feel the breeze from the ocean blowing on my face, and as I reached up, I noticed I had on a wide-brimmed beach hat that shaded me from the sun. That was odd; I never wore a beach hat. I loved the sun on my face.

Suddenly, Claudia let out a loud squeal. "OMG, Allie, what have you done?"

When I looked in her direction, she was also wearing an oversized beach hat. It was so large it also covered her face. Staring down at her hands, she was flipping them back and forth. She jumped up and started frantically spinning in circles, kicking sand in every direction.

"Oh no, look at me!" She lifted one of her legs, and the loose skin on her thighs resembled wrinkled crépe paper. Claudia lifted both her arms and spun in circles and cried out, "Just look at this! Where did my muscles go? The skin that hangs from my arms could be used as sails if we ever get lost at sea. I can just hear you now, '*Ahoy, Claudia, hoist your arms. We're going to turnabout. We're getting a strong headwind!*'"

When she finally stood still long enough, I started laughing so hard, tears were streaming down my face, and I couldn't speak.

"Oh, you think this is funny? You look like an old hag yourself, you know. You have so many wrinkles it's hard to tell where your face ends and your neck begins. It's a good thing you never wore heavy earrings like me, or you would probably have gigantic holes in your ears from the weight of them stretching your skin. Oh, my God, do I have big, loopy holes in my ears?"

Finally gaining control of my emotions, I stiffened my lips and cleared my throat. "Calm down, Claudia, you're fine! First of all, I didn't do this. You did! You're the one who took us here. I tried to talk you into waiting, but no, you wouldn't hear of it! You couldn't wait! You had to get right to traveling, right then and there."

I was trying hard to keep my laughter under control, but a slight giggle slipped out. "This is what can happen when we don't think things through! I told you to think of a place we spent time together when we were younger."

Claudia gave into the humor and let out a huge belly laugh. "I did! We have spent a lot of time here for the past several years."

"Yes, but you were supposed to think of a time and place, not just the place!"

Dropping her chin to her chest, with her best whining voice, she pleaded, "Okay, okay, I get it! Please, can we just go back to our own time? I don't like this look on us at all!"

Reaching out and lifting her head, I chuckled again. "That, I know how to do. Hold the chain so your pendant hangs in front of your face. Move it slowly back and forth, focusing on it while you think of your true time, and it will take you there."

Within seconds, we were sitting back on the floor in front of the fireplace. Brick was frantically barking and growling at the door as he paced the floor. The sound of a car speeding out and down the dirt driveway rang out over all of his commotion. Jumping to our feet, we ran to the front windows of the cabin, only to see a cloud of dirt that was settling back down in the wake of whatever vehicle had just raced out.

Taking Brick by the collar to calm him down, I walked him over to the leather couch. "It's okay, boy, settle down, it's okay."

Stepping away from the window, Claudia asked, "Is Emily here?"

"No, she's not. It would have been great if she was. Maybe she could have told us who that was."

"That's what I was thinking."

"Look, Claudia, let's have something to eat and get ready to move on. We need to get out of here as soon as possible. We have the pendant now. After all, that's what we came here for in the first place, right? We can't ever afford to become complacent. Over the past few days, I think we've become way too comfortable here, and that's dangerous. We can't ever let our guard down! It's important to keep moving forward with great momentum to gain the advantage of being on the offensive."

As we were finishing lunch, we heard a car pulling up the dirt driveway. As we looked out, we saw a large black truck with tinted windows pull up next to Claudia's SUV. As we watched, Miss Dawn climbed out of the vehicle, raced up on the porch, and began frantically banging.

Claudia grabbed the door, pulling it open as Dawn rushed in. "You girls need to get out of here right now!"

I flew across the room and slammed the door shut. "What? Why?"

"Because there was a man at the General Store about an hour ago. He was asking me all kinds of questions about that organ. He was also asking if I had seen or met a couple of women named Allie or Claudia? She spun frantically in my direction. "He claimed to be your fiancé!"

"Did you tell him we were there?"

"Absolutely not! He was so creepy! Emily was there, warning me the whole time. I told him nothing and got rid of him as quickly as possible."

I began pacing the floor. "Claudia, It could have been Josh."

Miss Dawn interrupted. "Well, that is the name he used. He said he was your fiancé, but Emily said no! It couldn't be your fiancé because she recognized the hoodie he was wearing. She said she thought it was the same guy she saw setting up the explosives at the little chapel. He was a big guy, with dark hair and dark piercing eyes. He was really menacing looking, and he definitely gave off an evil vibe!"

"Okay, Miss Dawn. Thank you for everything, but you really need to stay out of this from here on. This guy is extremely dangerous. We will take it from here. Besides, it's us he is after. We do have one small favor. Well, I guess it's a big one!"

"What is it? Just name it?"

"There are numerous law enforcement agencies after this guy. We have been working closely with them on this case in the past. In fact, we were under protective custody, but to be honest, we left the safety of that custody to go after him ourselves. I'm certain that Detective Payne from Stanford, Maine, who I currently work with, and other agencies will track Claudia and me down here soon. I don't want you to feel like you can't be honest with them. So please stay away from this cabin until we leave the area. That way, you can honestly say you met us and spoke with us, but you don't know how or when we left the area. Deal?"

"Deal! Be careful, you two. I don't know why you are going after him alone, but I'm sure you must have a good reason. In my mind, no one, but no one, would do that without good reason. I have a favor to ask as well."

"Okay, what's that?"

"When this is all over, can you both just let me know you're okay?"

Smiling, I reached out to offer a handshake. "That's a deal!"

Grabbing my hand, she pulled me over to Claudia. "Oh no, this deal deserves a group hug!"

"Okay, a group hug it is."

After we said our goodbyes, I placed my hands on Miss Dawn's shoulders, gently spun her around to face the door, and said, "Okay, go on then, get back to the General Store before Makya figures out you were here."

She immediately spun around. "Makya? Did you say Makya?"

"Yes. It just kind of slipped out. That's the name of the guy we are after."

"Well, let me tell you two, that guy is a bit of a legend around here. You know, he was in prison for quite some time. I have never laid eyes on the man, or at least not that I know of, but from everything I have heard, he's like a chameleon. He's Native American, and they say he takes on many personalities. He's like a Prince Charming one minute and a beast the next."

Throwing in her two cents, Claudia blurted out, "That's the guy all right! He really is pure evil walking. Allie and I suspect he's the one who planted the explosives in the church and showed up at your store today. Stay as far away from him as you possibly can. Whatever you do, don't make him angry!"

Chapter 27

As Dawn got in her car and drove away, Claudia and I sat down at the table. Brick came over, stood next to me, placed his head in my lap, and started whining softly. "What is it, boy?"

A voice from the loft above us rang out. "He's stressed!"

I looked up and then back down at Claudia. "Emily's back. She says Brick is nervous."

Claudia shivered. "I thought so; I could feel her. The temperature in here feels like it has dropped twenty degrees."

"You're right! You're getting great at sensing things, even when you can't see them."

Emily vanished from the loft, popping back into view at one of the cabin's front windows. "Talking about sensing things, Brick has a real instinct for knowing when someone is up to no good. That's why he is so stressed. He spotted and chased that freak out of here while you were both off on your little journey somewhere."

Standing, I marched over to her at the window. "You were here?"

"Ya, I was!"

"But when we found ourselves back in this room, the only one here was Brick. He was at the door growling and barking at some vehicle racing off down the driveway."

Claudia joined me at the window. "Come on, you two, this isn't fair. I can only hear half of this conversation!"

I raised my hand to quiet her. "Please, just give us a minute!"

Growing more anxious, Emily went on. "Yeah, well, that's because I followed him! He is one creep, all right! He went to the General Store and questioned Miss Dawn about you guys."

"Wait, do you know where he went after leaving the store?"

"Well, of course, I do! I didn't die yesterday, you know! I kept following him and found out that he made himself a great campsite about two miles from here. It's a perfect location at the base of a beautiful waterfall. I mean, if you think about it, it's rather ingenious! The falls provide fresh, clean water and a great fishing hole. Small game is plentiful there for hunting, and even better, he is just far enough away from this cabin to be undetected, but close enough to keep tabs on it."

Looking up, I spun in Claudia's direction and began pacing the floor. "That's great news!"

Claudia huffed and stepped in front of me so quickly that I ran right into her. "What's great? What the heck is going on? What did she say?"

"Geeze, sorry, it's not easy being the monkey in the middle, you know!

"Well, it's not easy being the odd man out either! What's the great news already? What is Emily saying?"

"It's Makya. He has a campsite about two miles from this cabin. He's expecting us, but he's really unsure where we are. Think about it, Claudia. If he's asking Miss Dawn about us, that must mean he hasn't really seen us yet. That also means he's not sure if it's us staying here at the cabin or if it's someone else. We need to pack up and get out of here before he figures that out."

"Yeah, that sounds all well and good, but where do you suggest we go?"

Emily popped in behind Claudia again. "Wait, you're leaving? What about Dolly? I thought you were going to help her."

"You're right, we did promise!"

Claudia spun around and walked right through Emily. "What did we promise?"

"We promised to help Emily's cousin Dolly."

"Look, Allie, I don't know how we can do that while we are trying to deal with Makya."

"Emily, Claudia's right, but I promise, as soon as we get through all this, we'll help Dolly. Even if we have to travel back here to do it."

Hanging her head in defeat, Emily drifted through the wall as her voice trailed off. "Okay, I truly hope so."

Claudia scanned the room as if she could suddenly see Emily. "Allie is a woman of her word. We'll be back!"

"I don't think she can hear you; she's gone. Come on, we've got to pack up and get out of here."

"Allie, just where are we going?"

"We need to set up camp somewhere."

"What? Make camp somewhere? You mean, like we used to with Grandfather, in the woods, with only a tent and a fire to keep warm at night?"

"Well, kind of. Why did you think we bought all these supplies? But, honestly, Claudia, we can't have a fire. It will give our location away."

"What? Are you kidding? We're going to freeze our behinds off! And I'm putting that nicely! Can we at least use the Coleman stove for cooking?"

"Claudia, that's why we bought the protein bars and other supplies. Besides, you know as well as I do, we can't be lugging a Colman stove with everything else we have to carry across this terrain."

"What about our cooler?"

"OMG! No, no cooler either! Now come on, if we get packing, we can get out of here why we still have a few hours of daylight. Maybe we can try to set up camp a couple miles from Makya. We're close enough to him now that maybe we can get the drop on him in the next few days. Especially since he isn't really sure exactly where we are."

We spent the next hour loading our backpacks and preparing for the next leg of our journey. I had even purchased a trail pack for Brick so he could carry his own supplies. We stashed everything we weren't taking with us in the attic crawl space to make sure we didn't leave any sign we had been there. Unless someone gained access to the cabin and searched it thoroughly, they wouldn't find any of our things.

Just before we headed out, I retrieved an area map we had purchased, opened it, and stretched it out over the table.

"Claudia, come here. Look, if I'm correct, based on Emily's description, this is Makya's position."

Moving my finger on the map about a mile upstream, I pointed to a second location. "See this spot? We can set up camp right around here, and I'm sure we won't have any trouble getting there before nightfall."

Picking up the map and the rest of our things, we headed for the door. "Brick, come on, boy, it's time to leave."

By four-thirty, we found a small clearing in the woods. Pausing, I pulled the map out of my pocket and unfolded it. "Well, will you look at this? A ready-made campsite, just for us!"

The humor certainly wasn't lost on Claudia as she slid off her backpack and dropped it to the ground. "Well, if it isn't the Camp Hilton!"

"Very funny! At least we don't have to clear it. Come on, let's set up camp."

As we settled in to get some sleep that night, Brick went into guard mode and lay down between us with his nose facing the entrance of the tent.

A few hours later, Brick's low, warning growl woke me. Opening my eyes, I found him standing on all fours at the edge of the tent, baring his teeth. Leaning up on one elbow, I whispered, "What is it, boy?" Panic set in when I reached over to wake Claudia. I could feel the adrenalin course through my veins as my panic level rose. Her sleeping bag was empty. Knowing I had to remain calm, I stopped, collecting my breath and thoughts. Seconds later, I heard twigs breaking under someone's feet outside the tent. I slowly reached into my backpack to retrieve my pistol. Brick bared his teeth again, and by his reaction, I knew who or whatever was outside the tent was not Claudia.

My instincts kicked in and I immediately went into autopilot. Grabbing Brick by the collar, I whispered, "Brick, out!" He immediately stopped growling, but remained standing on high alert.

Placing my hand in front of his face, I gave him the hand signal to lay down, and he immediately hit the dirt. Turning his head, he let out a soft cry, as if he was asking me to release him. Holding my ground, I reached out and grabbed his collar a second time, trying to calm him, whispering again, "It's okay, boy."

Suddenly, the stillness was broken when a beam of light swept across the tent wall, and something struck it on the same side. Getting to my knees, I slowly pulled back the opening of the tent, only to hear footsteps rushing away from the campsite. The tree cover in the woods blocked any light from the night sky, making it impossible to see.

Reaching back to attach Brick's leash to his collar and grab a flashlight, I stopped and took a deep breath. Moving out of the tent, I stood directly in front of it and used the flashlight to survey the immediate area. At a little more than a whisper, I called out, "Claudia? Claudia, are you there?" There was no response. I tried a little louder. "Claudia, where are you?"

Still nothing. How could this be happening? Why would she leave the tent? Especially without letting me know. Something was terribly wrong.

Brick was frantically sniffing at the ground. Following his lead, I moved with him, shining the flashlight around the area to see if I could locate what hit the tent. Brick took me right to it. A small sixteen-ounce insulated stainless steel waterproof cylinder canister was on the ground. I recognized it immediately, as Claudia and I had purchased some of them to carry in our backpacks for our food and drinks.

Picking up the container, I cautiously opened the lid. Inside was a folded piece of paper. Opening it carefully, I found Makya's calling card, as two black rose pedals fell out. I began reading the note. *Well, you finally made it here. I'm still hoping to join forces with you, but you know what I have to do if that isn't possible. You know the consequences! One of us must put the other to rest. Ado until we meet in the forest. Before we do, I would highly recommend you consider my offer!*

My thoughts immediately turned to Claudia. Where the hell was she? It didn't make sense that she would leave the tent without waking me. Was it Makya? Did he lure her from the tent somehow? No, that couldn't be right either. Brick would have been frantic. Knowing there was nothing I could do until daybreak, I tried to rest until then. Brick and I got back into the tent. Still on high alert, he lay down next to me, never taking his eyes off the tent opening. With the chill of the air hovering around us, I lay there for the rest of the night, dozing in and out.

Chapter 28

As the inside of the tent brightened with the daybreak, I sat up to get my bearings. Brick, still laying beside me, glanced back as if he were waiting for me to give him direction. It had been almost impossible to get much sleep, even with Brick there keeping watch. Reaching over, I ran my hand down his smooth, sleek back.

"Hey, Brick, how are you doing, boy? I bet you're hungry! We need to eat and get moving. Claudia could be anywhere by now."

I reached into his trail pack and grabbed a baggy with his dry dog food. Pouring it into his small bowl, I tried to entice him to eat. "Here you go, boy. I know it's not exactly what you're used to eating, but we need to keep up our strength. When this is over, I promise you, we will both have a gourmet meal fit for royalty."

Joining him, I reached into my backpack and pulled out a couple of protein bars. "Well, Brick, this isn't the most appetizing breakfast either. I have to confess. Claudia was right about this one. These bars might be nutritious, but they certainly aren't bacon and eggs. God, that sounds so good right now. Who knows, in our travels today, maybe we can do some foraging and collect some fresh berries?"

Getting up, I began gathering our things to pack them up. Brick looked up at me as if to say, *Hey, where's the rest of my breakfast?*

"Sorry, boy, that's the best I have for now. It looks like you're going to have to carry Claudia's backpack. I'll tell you what. I'll carry your trail pack and we'll strap her backpack on your back. What do you say, boy?"

Brick looked up at me, tipping his head in one direction, then the other as he made a short whining sound.

"Brick, I swear, sometimes I think you understand everything I'm saying to you."

Within a half-hour, we were ready to head out. As I reached down for my backpack, I heard someone running through the woods as the leaves and fallen twigs snapped beneath their feet. Looking up, I saw Emily's cousin, Dolly, enter the clearing. Stunned to see me, she stopped short to catch her breath. She was sobbing, her eyes were swollen and her cheeks were bright red as she stood there, shocked to see me.

As I took a step toward her, she turned to run. "Wait, Dolly, are you okay?"

Looking back over her shoulder, still poised to leap back into the woods like a scared doe, she blurted out with a puff of air, "What?"

Without taking another step, I reached out with my hand. "Are you all right? Wait, don't leave. Can I help you?"

"No, I don't think anybody can help me. It's too late for that. I have to go!"

"It's never too late for help. Please, stop! What are you running from?"

Still out of breath, she huffed. "I'm not running from anything! It's not like that at all. I'm running to something, not from something."

"Okay then, what are you running to?"

Putting her desperation on hold for a moment, she fell to her knees, and taking a deep breath, she blurted, "Somewhere to start a new life. One that's located as far from here as I can possibly get."

"I don't understand. What could be so bad? Why are you running like your life could depend on it?"

"Because my life just might depend on it. Someone has been stalking me. I don't know who he is, but about six months ago, he came to our cabin and threatened my dad."

"Threaten him? About what?"

"I'm not sure, but my dad was really nervous after kicking him off our property. I don't think I have ever seen him so angry. He said, 'Dolly, don't you ever speak to that man. I mean it! If you see him walking down the street, cross the road and avoid getting anywhere near him.'"

"Do you know what he wanted from your dad?"

"No, but about a month ago, my dad just disappeared."

"Did you call the sheriff?"

Panic welled up in her voice as she began rambling. "No, because the night before he disappeared, he came into my room and said he might have to leave for a while because his being there could put me in danger. He was going to have me stay with some relatives while he was gone. I was so scared. I begged him to tell me why he had to leave, but he wouldn't say. When I asked him to call the sheriff, he said no, he couldn't. I thought he might be in some kind of trouble with the law, but he reassured me he wasn't. He said it would be too dangerous to bring them in on whatever was going on. Nothing he was saying made any sense. After he left, I kept thinking everything would be fine and that he'd be back soon. Besides, it's just my dad and me now. If anyone found out I was alone at the cabin, they'd come and take me away because I'm only sixteen.

"About a week after my dad disappeared, I saw the man in town again. He was really creepy, and he began showing up everywhere I went. I've been running and hiding from him ever since."

"Do you think maybe your dad knew him? Did your dad tell you his name?"

"Well, I'm certain my dad knew him from when he was in the military. I overheard part of their conversation when the man showed up at the house. My dad was furious. I heard him say, 'No, Mack, I won't be a part of anything you're planning. We're not in Afghanistan anymore, and I am certainly not for hire.'"

"Wait, what did he call him?"

"I think he called him Mack."

Trying to keep her from going into flight mode again, I put my hands out in front of me, palms down, motioning for her to stay calm. "Dolly, this is really important. Think back. Did he call him Mack or Mak?"

Emily suddenly appeared next to Dolly, and in unison, they both asked, "Mak?"

Ignoring Emily, I asked again slowly, "Did he say Mak or Mack?"

"Well, now that you ask, I think it might have been Mak. I thought he just mispronounced the man's name."

Emily suddenly appeared directly in front of me. "Allie, you have to keep Dolly with you now! She's in real danger!"

"I can't."

Confused, Dolly responded, "You can't what?"

Realizing she couldn't see Emily, I paused, trying to come up with what would be an appropriate response. One that wouldn't scare her.

"Ah, I was just thinking out loud. Look, Dolly, I think this guy that has been following you is the same one I am after, and he is even more dangerous than you could possibly imagine. If you promise to listen to everything I say, I will let you stay with me."

"Are you kidding? You and me tracking and catching this crazy guy? Did I mention he is big and scary?"

"Listen, Dolly, if you come with me, I'll explain everything when we stop and set up camp tonight, but trust me, I can take care of both of us. I promise!"

Getting back to her feet, Dolly dusted off her legs. "No thanks, I'll take my chances on my own. I'm getting really good at running and hiding."

"So, how long do you think you can keep that up? I'm telling you; this guy is good! He has the ability to find you anywhere. It might take him a little time, but trust me; eventually, you will come face to face with him. Would you rather be alone or with someone you can trust?"

"How do I know I can trust you? I don't even know you."

I had to think quick. She was ready to tuck tail and run.

"Do you trust Emily?"

"What's Emily got to do with this?"

"I knew Emily, and she always trusted me."

Skepticism was rising in her voice. "You knew Emily? How did you know Emily?"

"I met her a while ago. We got to be good friends."

"That's crap. Emily is dead! I don't believe you!"

I was losing her. It was clear that she didn't know who to trust.

Emily cried out, "Tell her you know about the time she and I took a bus and snuck off to a concert at the Liberty Hall in Kansas City."

Taking a step back, I stood tall, challenging her. "Well, if I didn't know her, how do I know about the trip you both took on the bus to the Liberty Hall for a concert in Kansas City?"

The look on her face softened, and her posture relaxed ever so slightly as she spoke in a whisper, "What? Wait, how did you know that? No one but Emily and I knew about that. We never told a single soul."

"I'm sure, but she did tell me that in confidence."

Dolly shook her head as if she was clearing away the confusion. "Even so, why should I believe that a woman like you could go up against a guy like him? That's just crazy!"

"Look, your dad is missing, and so is my friend, Claudia. We don't have time to stand here and argue about it, so let me show you why we can do this together. Looking around, I spotted a rotted-out log on the ground about ten feet away.

"Watch."

Focusing on the log, I raised my arm, elevating it for a few seconds, and then let it drop back to the ground.

She panicked. "OMG, you're a witch! Stay away from me!"

"No, Dolly, I'm not a witch. I'm Native American, and I have many gifts that have been passed down from my ancestors. Look, I get it. Think what you want, but I don't have time for this. Either you're coming with me, or you're not."

Turning, I hooked Brick's leash to his collar. "I'm going. You can come with me or keep running on your own. It's your choice."

As I took a few steps forward, I heard her breath out a sigh. "Okay, if Emily trusted you, I suppose I can, too."

"Good, I'm glad you're going to take a chance on me."

I unstrapped Claudia's backpack from Brick's back and handed it to Dolly. Do you think you could carry my friend's backpack until we find her?"

"Sure, it certainly doesn't look very comfortable for the dog to be carrying."

"Thanks. His name is Brick. He has his own trail pack to carry, so that would be great."

Chapter 29

L ate that afternoon, Miss Dawn was busily preparing to close the General Store when three strangers walked in. As she moved from behind the counter to greet them, she sensed they were not there to do any shopping. The older gentleman slowly pulled out his wallet, opened it, and flashed his badge.

"Hello, my name is Detective Payne." He looked back over his shoulder and continued. "These fine gentlemen are Josh Sullivan and Detective Jake Carpenter. Would it be possible to speak with the owner of this store?"

Stepping a little closer, she reached out to shake his hand. "Well, this must be your lucky day. You're speaking to her. I'm Dawn. How can I help you?"

Josh stepped out from behind Payne. "We're looking for someone."

Payne's cell phone rang. Stepping away, he looked back. "Excuse me, I have to take this call."

Moving forward, Jake handed Dawn a photo. "Actually, we're here on official business. We're looking for the two women in this picture. You haven't seen them, have you?"

She took the picture, studying it for just a few seconds. "Why yes, as a matter of fact, I have. While they were in town, they stopped by to do some shopping."

Josh took a deep breath and bent over, placing his hands on his knees in relief. "Oh, thank God!"

As Jake turned to scan the store, he asked, "They came in to shop?"

"Yes. They thought we were still a true old-style general store. The type that sells everything from hardware to clothing."

Picking up a candle, Josh asked, "Could you tell us what they were shopping for?"

"They were looking for things to help with their stay, like food and cleaning supplies."

"Anything else?"

"Yes, they wanted some camping supplies, but we don't carry those things."

Josh turned to Jake, taking a deep breath. "That's not good. If they have camping gear, they could be headed anywhere in the Ozarks."

Turning to Dawn, Josh cranked his neck. "Do you know where they're staying?"

"Sure. Well, wait, I should rephrase that. I know where they were staying. They were at the old Callahan cabin on the lake, just a few miles from here. To be honest, I'm not sure if they're still there. The last time I spoke with them, they told me they weren't staying much longer but didn't say when they were leaving."

As Payne finished his call, he overheard Dawn updating everyone. Stepping back to the group, he shrugged. "I can put that question to rest. That was Sheriff Jefferies on the phone.

He met the rest of our team at the Callahan place. They're going through the cabin and combing the area as we speak. There seems to be evidence that someone has been staying there recently, but there is no one there now."

Dawn reassured them. "It was definitely the girls staying there. To be honest, I have been really worried about them. They told me they were after a suspect named Makya? That guy has always been trouble and is quite well known around here. In fact, everyone around here knows he was in prison for quite a long time. It seemed crazy that they would be going after him on their own, but there was no talking them out of it."

Shaking his head, Josh began pacing the floor. "Well, that sounds like Allie and Claudia, all right."

Payne handed Dawn his card. "Thank you so much. We'll be in touch, but in the meantime, if you think of anything else that might be important, please give me a call."

"Thank you, I sure will. Just let me know if I can be of any further help."

A young woman entered the store. "Excuse me, gentleman, this customer is here to pick up an order."

Motioning for Jake and Josh to follow him, Payne called out. "Come on, you two, we're heading over to the cabin to meet the rest of the team."

While en route, Payne looked up at Jake in the rearview mirror. "According to the sheriff, there have been several unusual events in town over the past month. Most recently, someone planted explosives in an old chapel not far from the cabin. It was a professional job for sure. It blew the small chapel to the ground. Call it a coincidence, but it would appear that it happened the same day Allie and Claudia came into town."

Wringing his hands in frustration, Josh let out a low growl. "Coincidence? I think not. Was anyone injured in the explosion?"

"The sheriff said that no one was in the chapel. That's what was so strange. According to him, it is only used in the summer when the seasonal residents are here. The rest of the year, it's empty. No one has a clue why that might have been the target of anyone. Certainly, not this time of the year."

As they pulled up to the cabin and got out of their vehicle, they found the Sherriff on the porch with Detectives Carl Johnson from New York and Hayln Deere from Colorado. Climbing the stairs to join them, Payne offered the sheriff his hand. "You must be Sheriff Jeffries?"

"Yes, sir, I am, and you must be Detective Payne?"

"I am. Thank you so much for meeting us out here. Have you found anything?"

Carl interjected. "Well, Payne, it looks like someone was here. We found some clothes and personal belongings upstairs in the crawl space. They didn't try very hard to hide them, but they were tucked away."

Stepping forward, Hayln turned to Josh. "It would be helpful if you and Jake could take a look at what we found and verify that they belong to Allie and Claudia."

Chapter 30

Dolly and I headed out that morning and backtracked to Makya's campsite. When we got within eyeshot of it, I stopped short, clenched my fists in frustration, blurting out in a whisper, "Shit!"

Dolly stepped up next to me and grunted, spinning in all directions. "Yup, sure looks like we missed him all right!"

"I guess I didn't expect him to be here this morning. I knew he would move on after he paid us a visit to our campsite last night. The question is, how much of a head start does he have on us? Knowing him, he likely set out last night after paying a visit to our site. He knows this area like the back of his hand, and although traveling in these woods after dark would be challenging, it wouldn't be impossible for him."

"Wait, you said our campsite. You were alone, right? I mean, except Brick."

"No, that's what I meant when I said my friend Claudia was missing. She was with me, but she just disappeared into thin air while I was sleeping."

"What?"

C.J. Carson

Pulling an elastic from my pocket, I tied my hair back and motioned Dolly to follow me. "Well, that's the million-dollar question. She just up and disappeared. And what's worse is I'm not even sure how she got out of our small two-person tent without me knowing it. I only hope she didn't decide to take another little trip without me. She promised she wouldn't do that again. Honestly, I don't think it's likely that she left the tent voluntarily, especially without letting me know."

Moving closer to the campsite, it became clear that Makya had been holding up there for a while. The ground was beaten down from the many times he had moved in, out, and around the camp. He had made himself quite the fire pit, and by the amount of ash that had built up, he had used it many times.

"Come on, Dolly. Let's comb the area and see if we can find any evidence that Claudia may have been brought here. I don't know how he did it, but I'm sure he's responsible for her being missing. We need to look for anything at all that Claudia may have purposely left behind for us to find."

After searching for about an hour, we found nothing. We couldn't find one trace of Makya or Claudia.

Picking up a long stick, Dolly began pushing the ashes around in the fire pit. "Well, one thing is for sure, he hasn't been here for hours. This fire is cold. What time did you say he was at your campsite?"

Moving closer to the fire pit, I paused to think. "God, it was in the early morning sometime. He must have packed up and, as he was leaving the area, came by and somehow abducted Claudia and stayed around just long enough to make sure I took the bait."

Dolly spun to face me. "What do you mean, 'took the bait?'"

"Let's just say he left me a message. A little clue."

"Clue? As in some sort of note?"

"Yes, a note and what you might say is his calling card. It's a long story, but he wanted me to follow him. I think that's why he took Claudia."

"Okay, Allie, it seems you know this guy pretty well. It sure seems like you have gotten under his skin and in his head as well."

I chuckled. "You could say that! I've known this guy longer than you could even imagine."

"Yeah, but my dad, he's pretty old, and he was in the military with him."

Knowing there was no time to explain why I might know Makya longer than her father, I said, "Well, that's a story for another day. We need to keep moving and figure out where Makya has gone."

"Allie, this guy has a good head start on us and could be anywhere by now. How do you suggest we go about finding him?"

"You're right, but look, these footprints are heading off toward my campsite. Let's follow them back and see if we can pick up his trail from there. My guess is that he didn't cover his tracks well because he wanted me to follow him."

Dolly laughed. "Follow him? Why do you think he would want you to follow him?"

"Honestly, that's another long story, but suffice it to say, he wants my help with some things. Become his partner in crime, so to speak, and I am not willing to do that."

"That's just plain crazy, Allie!"

"It sure is. The guy we're dealing with is a very powerful and dangerous man. I will never join forces with him, and it's my intention to put an end to his reign of terror. He has traveled across the country, terrorizing and killing women and sometimes men for many years, and I intend to stop him once and for all."

When we arrived back at my campsite, I was able to determine just what direction Makya had gone. Taking Dolly by the arm, I pointed to some fresh tracks. "Look, see here? Looking at these tracks, it's clear that he was not traveling alone once he left my campsite. He came in alone and left with a second person. Someone is traveling with him, and they are still on foot, at least here."

"Where did you learn all this stuff, Allie? I mean, tracking people and things?"

"Honestly, I didn't learn to track people, but I did learn to track game. My grandfather taught both Claudia and me to hunt. Part of that was tracking our game. We had to learn about stillness, patients, and clues as well. I am hoping Claudia will leave me some clues as they travel to help me track them."

"What kind of clues?"

"Anything really. A torn piece of cloth hanging on some brush or even a mark of some sort on a tree. She could also purposely break branches on bushes and point them in the directions they are moving."

"Wow, Allie, you guys were really well trained!"

"Yeah, but I just hope she remembers all we were taught."

"It looks like this Makya guy is staying close to the Trail of Tears. Wouldn't that mean he is heading east?"

"Yes, it sure does, and if I know Claudia, she will try to come up with ways to slow him down. Let's head out and see if we can close in on them. If we stay close to the road, we can probably make it about four miles east before we make camp tonight."

"Camp? We're planning to camp tonight?"

"Yes, unless you have a better idea, we will be tenting it tonight."

"Well, actually, I do have an idea. I mean, if you really think we'll make it that far. I have some friends who live a little over four miles east. If we get that far today, I'm sure we could stay with them tonight."

"All right then, let's see if we can make that happen! It would be great to spend the night inside a building. What would be even better is if we could sleep in a bed or at least on a couch or a cot."

"It would, and they have a beautiful ranch with horses, cows, and goats. I'm sure you'd love it and I'm sure we'd be welcome there."

Hiking my backpack up to readjust it, I called out to Brick. "Come on, boy."

"You, too, Dolly. Let's not waste any more time talking about it, and get going."

I stopped short about four hours later, sliding my pack from my back. "Time for a short break. Here you go, boy." Pulling Brick's thermos and bowl from his trail pack, I poured him a drink.

Unzipping my backpack, I grabbed two protein bars, handing one to Dolly. "Here, you need to keep up your strength."

"Mmm, my favorite!"

Placing my backpack on the ground and sat down on it. Dolly followed my cue and sat as well.

Pulling any loose hair away from my face, I pulled the elastic from my hair to re-secure it. "He is making this way too easy for us. It doesn't seem that he is trying to cover his tracks at all!"

Dolly laughed and began rambling. "It seems pretty clear to me! I mean that this Makya guy wants us to follow him. You did say he wants you to join forces with him. Maybe he wants you to follow him, but doesn't want you to actually catch up until he is good and ready. By the looks of this, it seems pretty clear that he wants you to find him, or maybe at least follow him."

"Dolly, you're brilliant!"

"What? I'm just thinking out loud. I would hardly call that brilliant."

"Call it anything you want, but I think you hit the nail right on the head. He's not just using Claudia to lure me, but as a bargaining chip as well. He's staying just out of reach for a reason. If threatening to hurt Claudia can force me to join forces with him, he will want me to find him. On the other hand, if for any reason he still can't convince me to join him, he will try to lure me into a trap of some sort. In his mind, having Claudia is a win-win!"

"Wow, I said all that?"

"Not in those words, but yes!"

Chapter 31

A s the day went on, we were getting closer and closer to Makya. The tracks were becoming fresher as we continued to follow his trail. It was becoming increasingly clear that he was moving fast enough to keep a safe distance from us and still traveling with someone else.

As the sun lowered to the west, I stopped. "Hey, Dolly, look over to your right. There's a narrow trail with fresh hoof prints. Are we getting closer to your friend's ranch?"

"Yes. Do you see where that trail leads to a clearing just up ahead? That leads to their place."

"Thank goodness. I was just going to tell you we needed to stop and set up camp."

As we moved over to that trail, we noticed that Makya's tracks merged with the hoofprints. The expression on Dolly's face as she turned to me was of concern. "Allie, this is not good, is it?"

"I'm afraid not."

We continued to follow the tracks up to the edge of the clearing. Putting my arm up to stop Dolly from moving any farther, I warned. "Wait, check this out! See how the footprints start to merge together here? They are no longer discernable. There was a struggle. Here, follow my steps and stay off the trail."

I moved a few more steps. "Look, one or both of them took a spill right here. See the handprints? There are several of them." Moving a few more steps, I pointed again. "There, see the footprints right there? They both got back on their feet and moved further into the clearing through the dirt. And ahead over there, they moved up that hill through the pasture. See how the grass is disturbed in the same pattern all the way up?"

"Gosh, Allie, you're really good at this!"

"Thanks! I have to say, I'm thrilled to see two sets of footprints moving away. That must mean that Claudia held her own and that Makya still wants to keep her alive and healthy. If not, he will lose the only bargaining chip he has right now."

"Allie, do you think he hurt my friends?"

"I really hope not, but we're about to find out. What's at the top of this hill? Does it level out or drop down into a valley again?"

"It drops down a little and then levels out. I wouldn't exactly call it a valley."

"All right, we're going up to see if we can get a look. When we're about ten feet from the top, we're going to drop to our knees and crawl the rest of the way to the top. This tall grass will serve as a great cover, Okay?"

"Okay."

After pulling my binoculars from my backpack, we headed up the hill. When we reached the top, we dropped to our bellies. Using the binoculars, I scanned the house first. All the blinds were down. As I checked the barn and the other outbuildings, I could see they were also closed up tight. Except for the horses and animals in the paddocks, there was no sign of life anywhere.

Dolly was getting impatient. "Allie, what do you see? Can you see anyone at all? How about in the house?"

"I don't see any signs of your friends. The animals are all outside and seem to be safe. Look, Dolly, I'm going down there."

Handing her the binoculars, I began instructing her. "Here, you keep these. I need you to keep a lookout from here. Stay here with Brick. No matter what happens, keep him with you, and don't let him out of your sight."

"Allie, why can't I come with you? You might need help."

Trying to avoid any more questions, I pulled a small canister of mace from my backpack. "Here, do you know how to use one of these?"

"Yes, but, Allie—"

Pulling out my pistol, I interrupted her. "Look, this is all the help I need. Right now, I need you to listen to me very carefully. Your job is to keep watch with the binoculars. Give me time to clear the ranch. Once I clear everything, I will stand on the porch and wave my arms over my head with the pistol in my hand. If you don't see the pistol, that means something is wrong, and you need to take Brick and get out of here as fast as your legs will carry you."

"But, Allie—"

"No buts about it! I mean it. If you don't see that gun, get the hell out of Dodge!"

"Okay! Okay, I get it!"

"Dolly, see all the trees spread out across the grounds?"

"Yeah."

"I'm going to carefully make my way from tree to tree, one at a time, using them as cover. I will make my way to the barn and outbuildings first to clear each of them. Then I will move to the house. Is there a back entrance? Or even better, is there a bulkhead that leads to the basement?"

"Yes, there is a back door and a bulkhead."

"Okay then, I'll try to enter the house through one of those. That may allow me to get in without being heard or seen."

As I started toward the ranch, Dolly whispered, "Allie, please be careful."

Looking back over my shoulder, I nodded and winked. "Sure thing!"

Making my way down and across the property, I reached the barn, and it was clear. Moving to each of the outbuildings, I continued to check and clear the property. Saving the worst for last, I made my way to the house. Keeping my back to the building, I made my way around it, listening at each window for any noise or voices, but there wasn't any sound coming from inside. Working my way around to the back door, I tried the handle. It was unlocked. Shit, I knew that could mean one of two things. First, no one this far out in the country ever locked their doors, or second, this was the way someone wanted me to get in. I was hoping for the first.

Turning the knob, I slowly pushed the door open, stepped in, and closed it quietly behind me. I stood in a small mudroom. Stopping with my back to the door, I listened. It was so quiet that I could hear a ticking clock on the wall just inside the kitchen. The boards creaked as I took a couple of steps across the hardwood floor. Holding my breath, I stopped and waited. Everything was still quiet. I took a second giant step, placing my feet down on the tiled kitchen floor. That was better. No creaking at all. Slowly moving around the room, I made my way to a wall that opened up to the living room and carefully peeked around the corner. From the length of her hair, a woman was sitting in a chair, with her back to me. From the tie-knots on the back of her head, it was clear she wore a blindfold and a gag in her mouth. Still keeping my back to the wall, I raised my gun and made my way around the room to face her. She appeared to be, maybe, in her thirties. The floor creaked again, causing her to struggle and whimper loudly through the gag. Without waiting for another second, I raced over, pulled down her blindfold, and pressed my index finger to my lips. The minute she laid eyes on me, she quieted immediately.

As I took the gag off her mouth, she gasped for air. "Oh, thank God! Thank you so much!" Tears were streaming from her swollen eyes. "Where the hell is that maniac? Are you a cop or something?"

"No, ma'am! Are you okay?"

As I removed the restraints from her wrists and ankles, she continued gasping. "I am now, thanks to you! How did you find me?"

"It's a long story, ma'am. Could you please give me a minute?"

Stepping out on the porch with my pistol in hand, I waved the all-clear to Dolly.

She immediately stood, began running with Brick, and made it to the house in mere seconds. Throwing herself into my arms, she cried out, "I was so scared. What took you so long?"

As the woman inside made her way to the door, she called out, "Dolly, is that you?"

Dolly ran to her, clasping her hands, crying out, "Liz, are you okay? Where's Maria?"

"I'm okay. Maria hasn't been here for a few days. She went to visit her mother in Kansas City. Please, both of you, come inside. Let's call the police."

Stepping over the threshold, I pleaded, "Please, before you do that, can we talk?"

Liz stood there in shock. "What? Why would we ever wait? That guy has already got about a six-hour head start and, in my Jeep, no less."

"Please, just give me ten minutes. If you still want to call the police, I won't object."

Liz turned to both of us. "When is the last time either of you had a decent meal?"

Dolly chuckled, and with that, all the tension left the room. "I can't speak for Allie here, but it's been about a week for me."

Liz and I both looked shocked.

"I don't know why you're both so surprised. I have been alone for a while now. The only time I've gotten a decent meal in maybe a month was when someone took pity on me and invited me over for supper or something."

Liz whipped up a meal for us, and we all sat down at the table. I picked up my fork, thought for a second, and then placed it back across my plate. "Liz, can you tell me if the guy who did this to you was alone?"

"I sure can. He wasn't, and he had some young woman with him. At first, I couldn't tell if she couldn't speak or if he just wouldn't allow her to.

"I guess I should tell you that he seemed really pleasant when he first got here. He told me that their car had broken down about two miles up the road. When he asked to use my landline to call a tow truck, I didn't give it much thought. I felt bad for them, so I invited them in, let them use my phone, and fed them some sandwiches, chips, and iced tea. It did seem odd that the young woman was clearly not speaking!"

As Liz continued, she started sounding farther and farther away. I could feel my eyes rolling around in their sockets, and my breathing changed as the anger built up inside me. Suddenly, the iced tea pitcher sitting on the counter across the room exploded, sending tea and ice flying. Liz jumped up from her chair. "Holy shit, what the hell just happened?"

When I looked up, I could feel the tears pouring down my face. Standing from my chair, I began sobbing. "I'm so sorry. Oh, my gosh, I am so sorry!"

Standing from the table, I ran for the door as Dolly cried out, "Allie, wait!"

I just kept going until I fell into the dirt driveway.

Right on my heels, they were right behind me. Taking me by the arm, Liz lifted me from the ground. "It's okay, Allie. Come back in the house."

As I stood, my knees and the palms of my hands were bloody, and muddy tears drenched my face. "I'm so sorry, you guys. I'm so scared for my friend. It's all my fault she is in so much danger."

Dolly took my other arm, and they walked me back into the house.

Liz took me to the kitchen, sat me down, picked the gravel out of my wounds, washed them, and then covered them. Kneeling in front of me, she took my chin in both her hands, lifted my face, and looked deep into my eyes. "It's okay, my dear. Our ancestors have brought you here. Maria and I have been expecting you. None of this comes as a surprise to me. You need something in your stomach and a good night's sleep. You'll be better in the morning, and only then can we continue this conversation."

After I was all cleaned up, Dolly took me to a spare bedroom, and Liz brought me some toast and chamomile tea she had prepared. "Here, Allie, the toast is light, and the tea will help relax you so you can sleep. We can talk more in the morning, but only if you feel up to it."

I was so tired, drained, and exhausted, all I needed was that tea to help me get to sleep. In fact, I slept through the night until seven o'clock the next morning!

Chapter 32

I woke the next morning to the aroma of coffee brewing and cinnamon wafting from the kitchen. As I sat up, I found a robe laying across the bottom of my bed. Sliding it on, I followed the wonderful aroma coming from the kitchen, and when I got there, I found Liz and Dolly busily making breakfast.

Liz greeted me in the doorway with a mug. "Feeling better?"

Taking it from her, I lifted the mug to my face, took in the smell of the freshly brewed coffee, and took a sip. "Oh, yes, I am now. This is just what I need! Thank you so much!"

Dolly was on the opposite side of the kitchen, flipping pancakes on the griddle. "Are you hungry?"

"Honestly, I'm famished!"

Within a few minutes, Liz refilled my coffee, and we were sitting down to a fantastic breakfast!

I took my first bite and hesitated. "Hmmm!"

Dolly gasped and reached out as if she would take my plate. "Oh no, are they all right?"

Swiping her hand away, I smiled. "Hey! What? Are you kidding? These pancakes are delicious. I think they're the best I've ever eaten. They are so light and fluffy on the inside, yet they have a little bit of crunch on the outside. Great job, Dolly!"

"Thank you! I've been sworn to secrecy for fear of life or limb! My dad taught me our family's secret recipe."

After taking another sip of my coffee, I set down my mug. "I fear I owe you both a huge apology!" Turning to Liz, I smiled. "And I also owe you a new iced tea pitcher."

"Nonsense, I have three more just like it."

"Just the same, I am so very sorry about what happened last night. It's just that—it's just that I was so tired and I'm so scared for my friend Claudia. She's like a sister to me! I really need to get back on the road, but before I do, I need to know exactly what happened while Makya was here. Do you know who the girl with him was? Is she okay? Did he leave with her?"

Pouring herself another cup of coffee, Liz hesitated before turning back to the table. "Whoa, slow down. I'll be happy to tell you about it, but only if you promise not to wind yourself up again."

"I'll be fine."

"Okay, let's see, where was I? I was about to tell you that the woman with him wasn't talking. It wasn't clear if it was out of fear or if she just didn't have the ability to talk at all."

"Why did you think she might be scared?"

"Well, to start, she wouldn't make eye contact with me almost the entire time. Her demeanor was strange. She looked like a scared animal that was ready to bolt at any second.

148

"After they were here for a while, I tried to make small talk. I asked the gentleman what his name was, but he acted like he didn't hear me. I tried again, but again he totally ignored the question. He didn't even speak. I began thinking that maybe he was hard of hearing.

"The young woman finally spoke up. As she spoke, the rage and anger in her voice were palpable. 'Makya. His name is Makya.'

"He immediately looked up with such rage; his face turned crimson and then purple. I have never seen anyone so angry in my life. He stood immediately and flew across the room. Before anyone could react, he backhanded her so hard that I thought he might snap her neck. That single blow knocked her to the floor. I just stood there, paralyzed for a few seconds. I couldn't move. When I finally tried to help her up, he pulled a gun, shoved it in my face, and told me to sit down at the table.

"Suddenly, there it was, his true nature! He began pacing the floor, yelling at us. 'Now look what you've gone and done. This is all your fault.'

"The next thing I knew, he was hovering over the young woman. He grabbed her by the hair, pulling her to her feet, dragging her over to the front door. He stood there, yelling at her, but I couldn't make sense of anything he was saying. He was just babbling on and on. Finally, he opened the door, pushed her through it, and followed her out.

"Honestly, I didn't know what to do! I didn't want to make the whole situation worse by confronting him again. I could hear him continue to escalate outside. 'Now, look what you've done. You're supposed to be my bait and ace in the hole. Just look at you! You look like a war victim! If Allie lays eyes on you like this, she'll never work with me. Do you know what that means? I'll have to kill her, which will be all your fault!'

"It went silent for several seconds, and then I heard what I think was the girl falling down the stairs! That was the last time I laid eyes on her. In seconds, he came back into the house and asked for the keys to my Jeep parked in the driveway. After I retrieved them for him, he tied me up and left. A few minutes later, I heard him start up the vehicle, pull it up to the house, throw her in the Jeep, and speed off."

Getting up from the table, I stepped over behind Dolly, placing my hands on her shoulders. "I need to get moving, and you need to stay here at Liz and Maria's. That bastard Makya is escalating. We can't even be certain if Claudia is still alive!"

"But, Allie, you said you would keep me with you! I told you, I want to get as far away from here as possible! You promised!"

"Dolly, I gave you my word. If that's truly what you want, I will come back for you!"

Turning back to Liz, I took a deep breath and puffed out the air. "Last night, you said that our ancestors had brought me here. That you and Maria had been expecting me. You said that my coming here and all the events that are happening, as a result, did not surprise you. Can I ask you to explain that to me? Are you Native American? Do you have a gift for seeing or knowing things?"

"Slow down, Allie, no! Actually, I'm Scottish. It's my ancestors that warn and protect me from impending danger."

"Oh, I thought—"

She sighed. "Don't concern yourself with that for now, my dear. For now, you aren't in any immediate danger, and you have a lot of ground to cover when you leave here."

"You're right! I have no idea how I will catch up with them now that he has your Jeep. I guess I will have to backtrack, get the SUV that Claudia and I used to get us to the cabin in the first place, and then go after him from there."

Liz stood up. "There is no time for that. Grab your backpacks and Brick, follow me."

After making our way across the yard, Liz stopped with a massive grin! "Have I got some wheels for you!"

Turning, she stepped up to the barn and began pushing its huge door to the right, exposing its massive interior.

Reaching in, switching on the light, she handed me a key and chuckled. "Here you go!"

"What is this?"

Pulling me to the other side of the barn, she gloated. "You'll see!"

We stopped just outside an oversized standing stall. Stepping just inside, she grabbed a large canvas sheet and pulled it to the ground. Sitting there was a cherry red '68 Ford Mustang hardtop convertible. Turning, she grinned and bragged. "She's souped-up, gassed up, and ready to go!"

"Are you kidding?"

"No, this is just what she's made for. She's fast and in amazing condition!"

"Oh no, I couldn't!"

"You have to. A car can always be fixed or rebuilt. We don't have time to stand here and debate this. Your friend is in danger, and you need a way to catch up with that maniac."

Reaching up, I wrapped both my arms around her neck. "Thank you! Thank you so much! Please take care of Dolly. When this is all over, I'll be back with your car, hopefully in one piece!"

"Just save your friend and stop this guy!"

As I went to open the car door, something compelled me to look up. Right above me, on the beam over the stall, was what looked to be a crossbow and a long leather bag. Turning to Liz, I gasped. "Is that what I think it is?"

"It's a latch!"

"A latch? No, I mean the crossbow!"

"Well, yes, but we call it a latch in Scotland."

She pulled down the bow and the leather bag, handing them to me. "It belonged to one of my ancestors. I couldn't even begin to guess how old it is."

Pulling a shaft out of the leather bag, I examined it. "Looks like some sort of an arrow to me?"

Reaching down in the bag again, I counted. "And look here, there are six of them."

Liz looked puzzled by my reaction. "Six? Does that have some significance?"

"It certainly does. I just happen to have six arrowheads with me. Arrowheads that were kept for years in an ancestral box I inherited from my grandfather. But that's a story for another day."

"Take these with you, then! I believe there are no such things as coincidences!"

"My thoughts exactly."

Dolly came running into the barn, holding Bricks trail pack. "Don't forget this!"

"Thank you. We will definitely need that."

Liz threw a small cooler and thermos on the back seat as we loaded up the car. "There are some sandwiches and fruit in the cooler and fresh coffee in the thermos."

Opening the passenger door, I summoned Brick. "Come on, boy, we've got to go."

Turning, I gave Liz and Dolly each a massive hug before climbing into the driver's seat. "Take care of yourselves."

Chapter 33

As I pulled out of the barn and down the driveway, a familiar voice rang out in the back seat. "Thank you so much for getting Dolly to a safe place."

Glancing up in the rearview mirror, Emily was smiling back at me. "You're entirely welcome, but what the heck are you still doing here? I thought you were here to make sure Dolly was safe? She's fine now. Shouldn't you be moving on? I don't think I need anyone else getting in the way."

"One would think that, but clearly, my work here isn't done. I must still have something I need to do!"

"Like what?"

"Oh, I don't know! Like maybe to help keep you on Makya's trail. After all, it's going to be virtually impossible to track him in any old conventional way. Especially now that he's no longer on foot. Wouldn't you agree?"

"Well, you have a point there, but you don't have to be so smug about it."

She burst out laughing. "Smug? Was I being smug? Look, you need my help, whether you want to admit it or not. Just think about it; I'm the perfect sidekick. He can't kill me. Heck, he can't even hurt me. I'm already dead!"

"Sorry, you're right! I don't even know where to begin looking for him. I suspect he is moving east. I think he's following the Trail of Tears."

"You're right, he is, but he's still about six hours ahead of you. The odds of you catching up with him aren't really in your favor. Not unless he stops intentionally to let you catch up, but I can tell you one thing for sure."

"Okay, I'll bite. What can you tell me?"

"His last stop was at an excellent little family-owned diner in Hopkinsville, Kentucky. It's called Jennie's Place.

"And you know that how?"

"Because I followed him there, of course. I would check that place out if I were you."

Pulling off the road to set my GPS, I asked, "You said Hopkinsville, Kentucky, right? Right?"

She wasn't answering because she was gone. I looked in the rearview mirror to see Brick staring back at me. "Well, I guess it's you and me for now, boy. Let's just hope she's gone to wherever Makya is to keep an eye on him because once again, she has flown the coop!"

Heading east, I traveled about four hours on Route 68, trying to stay as close to the Trail of Tears as possible. I finally spotted a sign that read: 5 miles to Hopkinsville. The timing couldn't have been better because I needed gas, and I was getting hungry. Brick and I had already eaten the sandwiches Liz had packed in the cooler.

As soon as I got into town, I found a gas station to fill my tank. There was a young man at the pump next to me. Pulling off his cap, he wiped his forehead with his sleeve and then looked up. "Good mornin', ma'am."

"Good morning, and how are you on this fine sunny day?"

"To tell you the truth, ma'am, I'm feelin' a bit of heatstroke. I've been workin' out there on the tractor all mornin' long. I had to take a noon break just to get out of the sun."

"I'm looking to take a break from driving myself. Would you happen to know of a little diner in town? I think the name of it is Jennie's Place."

"Yes, ma'am, I do. If you're lookin' for some great home cookin' that sticks to your ribs, that's the place to go. Best fried chicken, biscuits, and gravy ever! It's just down the road a bit on East 6th Street."

"That sounds like just the place for me to grab a quick meal."

As I reached out to shake his hand, he withdrew a bit. "I don't mean to be rude, ma'am, but I am a bit sweaty and dirty to be shakin' your hand."

"I appreciate your thoughtfulness. That's not rude at all. It's actually a bit gallant. Thank you for the information about the diner. Have a good day."

A few minutes later, I pulled up to the restaurant. Parking the car, I locked the car and left air conditioning in the car running for Brick. "I'll be back in a bit, boy. You keep an eye on things while I grab something to eat."

As I entered the little diner, a friendly young woman greeted me. " Good afternoon. Is there anyone with you today, or will it be a table for one?"

"It's only me today. I can eat at the counter. Please, save your tables for other parties."

"Sure, follow me."

As I took my seat, the young waitress handed me a menu. "Here you go, ma'am. My name is Meghan. Can I get you something to drink while you look over the menu?"

"That would be great! I would love an unsweetened iced tea with lemon. I hear you have the best fried chicken, biscuits, and gravy ever! Is that true?"

"Why yes, ma'am. I mean, I don't like to brag, but that's what they do say! Our mashed potatoes are pretty amazing as well."

"Well, then I don't think I need this menu. I'll just trust the recommendation I was given and have the fried chicken and everything that comes with it!"

"Sure thing! I'll put that order right in and bring your iced tea right over."

Within ten minutes, Meghan brought my plate and placed it on the counter in front of me. When I saw the dish, my eyes grew to the size of saucers.

She smiled. "Looks good, huh?"

"Yes, and it smells even better than it looks."

As she walked away, I looked up. "Excuse me, Meghan?"

Stopping, she turned. "Yes?"

Pulling a photo of Claudia and me from my purse, I asked, " Could you do me a favor? Actually, two favors?"

"Sure, what do you need?"

"Well, first, I have a starving dog in the car. Do you think I could get a couple of burgers without the rolls to go for him?"

"Absolutely! That's an easy one, and what else do you need that I can help you with?"

Holding out the photo, I asked, "Could you take a look at this? Have you seen the girl that's in this photo with me?"

Carefully studying the picture, she pursed her lips and began shaking her head. "No, I don't think so."

"Please look again. Are you absolutely sure?"

"She would have been in here either yesterday afternoon or early this morning."

"I'm sorry, ma'am. She doesn't look familiar. But, to be honest, I was off yesterday. Can I show this to the owner? She's here every day."

"Of course."

Meghan took the photo with her through the swinging door to the kitchen. Within seconds, another woman bolted back from the door, headed directly to the counter, stopped right in front of me, and blew out, "Excuse me, Ma'am, but is this your friend?"

It took me a few seconds to compose myself enough to answer. "Yes, OMG, yes. Her name is Claudia. She was here, wasn't she?"

"Yes, ma'am, she was! Yesterday, just as I went to lock the door and close the diner, that poor girl came in with some guy. I would typically tell anyone coming in at that time that we were closed for the day, but I couldn't shake the feeling that something was terribly wrong. I remember thinking, this girl looks like she is in some sort of trouble. To tell you the truth, I think she is sick or something. She did not look good at all, and she barely ate anything. I was hoping she would use the restroom while they were here. I thought maybe I could send someone in there to see if she was okay, but she never left her seat the entire time they were here. She never spoke a word, not even to the guy she was with. She just sat there at the table, looking down at her plate."

I could feel myself growing angrier and angrier by the second. "I bet he never left her alone either, right?"

"No, not at all. At one point, I thought he might. He got up and left her sitting there, but he came directly to me and asked for the bill, never letting her out of his sight. While they were eating, I went back to the kitchen to call the police, but before they could get here, he paid the bill, and they left."

Standing from the counter, I slipped the photo back into my purse. "I'm sorry, I didn't get your name. Are you Jennie, the owner of this diner?"

"Yes, I am, and I'm so sorry we couldn't get your friend, Claudia, the help she needed fast enough. When the police officer did get here, he told us that there wasn't anything they could do under the circumstances."

"I understand. I am just so grateful you were able to serve Claudia and get her to eat something. Even if it was just a little."

As we talked, Meghan came out of the kitchen with my check and to-go order, setting them down on the counter.

Taking cash from my purse, I handed it to her. "Thank you for that delicious meal and all your help. I am so grateful to know that Claudia was here.

Chapter 34

That same afternoon, Liz and Dolly were out on the front porch, enjoying a late lunch. Suddenly, Sheriff Jeffries' cruiser and three unmarked vehicles came racing up the long dirt driveway with their lights flashing.

Without turning her head, Liz said under her breath, "I'll handle this, Dolly. Unless they address you directly, don't say anything."

Liz stood and cheerfully greeted them as they approached the porch. "Good afternoon, Sheriff."

"Good afternoon, Liz."

He removed his hat and climbed the stairs to the porch. "Dolly, where in tarnation have you been? We've been searching all over for you."

"I've been here."

Liz interrupted. "Her father left her with Nancy and me while he was out of town on business. My guess is that is not why you came here with a whole army of law enforcement, is it?"

"Well, no—"

"Hello, ma'am, my name is Detective Payne. We're sorry to bother you on this beautiful day, but we are looking for a couple of young women." As he moved up to the porch, he turned and continued. This is Detective Jake Carpenter and Josh Sullivan.

Handing her a picture he took from a folder in his hand, he inquired, "Have you seen either one of these women?"

Without hesitation, she smiled. "Well, as a matter of fact, I have. They were actually both here yesterday."

Josh took a step forward. "Both of them? When did they leave?"

"Well, the two women weren't traveling together. One of them was here with a man. I believe his name was Makya. They left early yesterday. The other woman said her name was Allie. She got here later in the day, stayed here last night with Dolly and me, and then headed out this morning."

Confused and panicked, Josh climbed the stairs to join Payne and Jake. "What? How is that possible? Claudia would never join forces with Makya!"

Dolly interrupted, blurting out, "Claudia wasn't with him voluntarily. That guy was crazy. He forced her to leave with him."

Payne closed his eyes and dropped his head, driving his thumbs across both his temples in a circular motion to release some tension. Then, looking up, straight into Liz's eyes, he said, "Okay, I don't know what you may have promised Allie to buy her time, but we need to talk. It's unreasonable for her and Claudia to be chasing this guy all over the country by themselves. They're already running into a heap of trouble from the sounds of things."

Shrugging, Dolly sheepishly looked up at Liz, who was already staring back at her in a disapproving manner.

There was no use trying to cover anything up now. Dolly had let the genie out of the bottle. "Of course, gentleman, come in."

Stepping into the ranch house, Liz offered everyone a seat. "Can I make some coffee, or would anyone like a cold drink?"

Chapter 35

Leaving Jennie's Diner, I made my way back to the car. Brick was sitting in the front passenger seat, anxiously awaiting my return. As I unlocked and opened the car's back door, he jumped into the back seat. His little stub of a tail started wagging as he sat patiently to see if the food I had in that great smelling takeout bag was for him.

"What a good boy, Brick. You have better manners than some humans I know."

Reaching into the sack, I pulled out the contents and opened the container. "Wow, boy, they sent you quite a treat. Much more than I even asked for!"

As I sat the container down on the seat, Brick looked down at it and then back up at me.

"It's okay, boy, it's all yours."

He immediately dove in and devoured it in just a few seconds. Lifting the empty container from the seat, I took a deep breath and huffed out, "Wow, you didn't even come up for air! I think you just earned a lifetime membership from the clean plate club. It looks like you enjoyed the food from Jennie's as much as I did."

After climbing into the driver's seat, I pulled out my cell phone to check Google search results. "Well, Brick, I guess we'll just keep heading east, and where is Emily when you need her, anyway? Huh, boy?"

"I'm right here, and girl, you need to get a move on!" And there she was, sitting in the front passenger seat.

"Well, hello there, stranger! Do you have an update for me?"

"Stranger? You're kidding, right? And by the way, I hope you enjoyed that meal you had at the diner because we need to make up some time. No more stops until you get to The Stanley Inn."

"The Stanley Inn?"

Turning with excitement bubbling from her entire being, Emily repeated, "Yes, The Stanley Inn, in Marietta, Georgia. Makya has checked in there. Hopefully, for the night, and it's only five hours from here! I overheard him talking to the woman at the desk. He told her he was headed to Murrells Inlet in South Carolina. Then once they got to their room, I heard him tell Claudia he was meeting some old drunk named Jack there."

"That's great!" Checking the Google app, I entered The Stanley Inn, Marietta, Georgia. "There it is! You're right; it's just about five hours from here.

I looked up, and once again, Emily was gone. "Geeze, Brick, she doesn't stick around long, does she?"

Before heading out, I called ahead and made a reservation. After hanging up, I turned to Brick, "Well, boy, it looks like you'll be camping out in the car tonight. They don't allow pets at the Inn. Don't worry, I only plan to sleep a few hours."

I drove four and a half hours without stopping when Brick sat up in the back seat and whined. Looking ahead, I saw the sign: Marietta, 15 miles.

Pulling into the first gas station I could find, I parked, got out of the car, and hooked Brick up to his leash. "I don't know about you, but I can't drive one more mile without stretching my legs. Come on, boy, let's take a walk."

Moving from the car, I walked over to an open field next to the parking lot. There was another woman there, walking a tiny, fluffy black puppy. Knowing how intimidating Brick's appearance could be, I stepped up from the curb onto the grass and stopped, keeping my distance. Brick sat down at my feet, looked up at me, and then looked at the small dog.

Smiling, the woman greeted me. "Good evening. That sure is a well-trained and mannerly dog you have there."

"Thank you. His name is Brick, and my name is Allie. That is an adorable little puppy you have there."

"Thank you. I'm Terry, and this little girl is Zoey. My husband and I just got her yesterday. We haven't even had her long enough for her to learn what her name is."

"Well, she's adorable."

As we talked, the tiny puppy wiggled her way out of her collar and started running off. Terry screamed and ran after her.

Trying to help, I called out, "Wait, don't chase her. She'll come to you if you just get her attention and then run away from her."

It was too late. Terry was already panicking and didn't really hear a word I was saying. Brick stood and began pacing in place, looking up at me, waiting for me to release him.

I unhooked his leash and pointed in the direction that Terry was running. Within seconds, he ran past Terry and caught up with Zoey. Picking her up by the scruff of her neck, Brick gently carried her back to Terry, dropping the tiny black ball of fur right at Terry's feet. Kneeling down, Terry scooped Zoey up, cradling her in her arms.

When I got to them, Brick was standing right in front of Terry, wagging his tail, and awaiting direction. I called out, "Brick, heel!"

He immediately ran around me and sat at my side. Kneeling down, I gave him a big hug. "Good boy, Brick! You're such a good boy!"

Terry stood and approached Brick. "What an amazing dog! Is it okay if I pat him?"

"Sure, he loves pats and hugs."

After smothering Brick with lots of gratitude, Terry stood up. "You're not from here, are you?"

"No, I'm just passing through. I am actually looking for the Stanley Inn?"

"It's not far from here, just a few miles up the road. It's a beautiful place. My husband, Jack, and I actually had our wedding reception there. But wait, they don't allow pets."

"I know. He is really a good boy. Brick will have to spend the night in the car. I think he'll be fine."

"No, we can't have this sweet dog sleep all night in the car. Look, call it a coincidence, but I have a doggy daycare and boarding facility in Marietta. It's called Littles Playhouse. I would love to put Brick up for the night. It's the least I can do for him since he saved Zoey and all. Come on, what do you say?"

"First, I always say there is no such thing as coincidences, and second, I say, how can I refuse such a generous offer? That would be great!"

"Okay then, why don't you follow me into town? We'll get Brick checked in to my place, and then you can go to get checked into the Inn."

Chapter 36

It was close to seven o'clock when I arrived at the Stanley Inn. As I drove up to the building, it did not disappoint. It was every bit as beautiful as the pictures depicted in their brochure on the Internet. Pulling into the parking area, I saw no sign of the Jeep that Makya was driving, and I knew instantly I had missed him again. Parking the car, I grabbed my duffle bag and made my way up the walkway to the entrance.

Stepping through the doorway, a petite, soft-spoken woman with a strong Georgian accent greeted me. "Good evening! Welcome to the Stanley House. Are you Miss Allie Callahan?"

"Hello, yes I am."

"Please come in. We've been expecting you. It's so nice to meet you. Can I get someone to help you with your things, dear?"

"No, I'm fine. All I need this evening is this one bag, but thank you for asking."

"Well then, honey, let me take you upstairs. We've reserved the Buckhead room for you."

Following her up to the second floor, I asked, "Could you recommend a good place to eat that's close by? Somewhere I could get something lite to eat?"

As we approached the top of the stairs, she turned. "There are several fine places to eat, but I recommend the Marietta Diner. Eating there is simply an experience all by itself, and honey, they have something for everyone. If you are looking for a lite meal, perhaps a salad or soup, you can get it there. I promise you will just love the place. It's not far from here, and even better, it's open twenty-four hours."

"That sounds perfect."

"I'm glad I could help, and trust me, honey, you're in for a treat."

Stepping up to one of the doors in the hallway, she reached out. "Here's your room. I hope you enjoy your stay with us. We serve breakfast every morning from seven a.m. until noon. Is there anything else I can help you with?"

"Yes, just one more thing. Could you give me a wake-up call tomorrow at seven?"

"Why sure, darlin'! No problem, seven it is. Are you sure there is nothing else?"

Opening the door, I stepped into the warm and inviting Victorian room. Its high ceilings gave the room a spacious feeling, and it was beautifully decorated with a king-sized bed, an ornamental fireplace, and warm hardwood floors. Near the fireplace, a large slipper-shaped soaking tub was tucked in one of the room's corners. A soak in that tub was definitely on my to-do list as soon as I got something to eat.

"This is just perfect! I don't think I will need anything else at all. Thank you."

Placing my bag on the floor next to the bed, I picked up my phone to check the GPS for the Marietta Diner. I discovered it was three miles from the Inn. It was close, but still too far for me to walk, given how tired I was.

Getting in the car, I drove to the diner, and when I pulled into the parking lot, I realized exactly what Madison meant when she said I would enjoy the experience. It was like I had gone back to when old-time diners with shiny exteriors were commonplace, but with one big difference. This wasn't just your typical old-style diner. It was not just a restaurant at all. It was a destination place, and it was large and in charge. The restaurant was the experience before you even sat down at a table or ordered your food. The minute I entered the large front entry, I was engulfed in the luxury of lighted ceilings with old-style fixtures and rows of booths and tables. I knew having a lite meal at this great diner was no longer an option. To truly get the full experience of this amazing diner, I would have to order one of their many magnificent dinners, so that's exactly what I did. After reading the menu, I decided on the Broiled Sea Scallop dinner with a slice of coconut cream pie for dessert.

As I sat there enjoying every bite of that fantastic dessert, it occurred to me I had actually been able to sit there and just enjoy my meal with no interruptions from Emily or anyone else. I couldn't easily explain it, but the mere quietness of that moment made me feel uncomfortable, like experiencing the calm just before the storm.

Dropping my fork in my dish, I raised my hand to catch the waitress's attention and asked for my check.

Leaving the money and check on the table, I immediately headed to the door.

Stepping out of the diner, an eerie feeling was in the air. A sudden chill ran down my spine as all the lights on the entire street went out. As I gazed up at the sky, it had taken on a grayish purple tint, and although the atmosphere was calm and unusually still, rolling black clouds were moving quickly overhead. Suddenly, nothing was moving except me. Everything had stopped. The people walking on the streets looked like mannequins, and the car's engines were silent. Across the street was a child with a ball suspended mid-air while the child remained motionless.

Then, a familiar voice rang out behind me. "Hey, Allie, catch me if you can!"

Turning around, Makya was standing on the other side of the parking lot before he disappeared.

"No, Allie, I'm over here!"

Spinning around, Makya was standing on the opposite side of the street.

As my anger grew, so did the sarcastic grin on my face.

Pointing to the pavement directly in front of me, I challenged him. "Why don't you try that again, but from over here? What, are you afraid I might whip your ass?"

Within a blink of an eye, he stood in front of me. "You mean right here?"

Taking a swing at him, my fist passed through him.

"Nice try, Allie! Don't you remember this trick? You used it on me years ago. Well, on a version of me, when I was Calian. I'm not really here. We're both suspended in time, mere holograms of ourselves!"

"Oh, I remember, all right!"

"Allie, look up. There's a storm brewing."

Standing in the middle of the road, listening to Makya, a voice that seemed far off in the distance called out to me. "Hello, Miss. Hey, ma'am, are you all right?"

Abruptly, everything was moving again. A young man holding a piece of paper was standing in front of me. "You forgot your receipt, ma'am."

A bit shook, I tried to speak. "Ah, thank you?"

"My name is Robert, ma'am, and you're welcome. Are you okay?"

Shaking my head to clear the cobwebs from my head, I looked at him. "I'm fine. Thank you for bringing this out to me. That was so kind."

As Robert returned to the diner, he looked over his shoulder. "You're welcome. I hope you join us again."

When I headed to my car, a chill ran down my spine when something occurred to me: I sensed Makya coming. He was trying to unnerve me, and I would not let him get away with it. I needed a good night's sleep, and I was going to try to get it.

After returning to the Inn from eating, I began filling that amazing tub with warm water. In the bathroom, on a table next to the shower, I found various soaps, bottles of shampoo, and a small container of bath salts. Moving back to the tub, I drizzled the bath salts under the faucet, allowing them to dissolve and spread through the water.

Knowing I couldn't relax unless my burner phone was within arm's length, I pulled a tall stool next to the tub to rest it on while I bathed. Pulling my hair up, I tied it in a tight bun on top of my head. Stepping into the warm tub, I slid down, submerging myself up to my neck. The surface steam from the lavender-scented liquid filled the air. Closing my eyes, I slid down until the warm water closed in around my face, and my racked-with-tension body, melted into a deep state of relaxation.

After soaking in that warm bath for about forty minutes, I looked down at my hands. They were looking wrinkled, reminding me of that first traveling experience attempted by Claudia when she brought us to the beach to our future ripe old ages. A smile crept over my face as I remembered how ridiculous she sounded as she danced around in the sand, remarking on how horrible we looked like our future selves.

As the water cooled off, I climbed out of the tub and slipped into the shower to wash my hair. After releasing all that tension, my body felt weighted from the exhaustion, and my eyelids were too heavy to keep open. The king-sized bed was calling out to me, and I abided. As I climbed into bed and buried myself in the cozy bedding, I fell asleep.

Sometime later, the sound of war drums in the distance jarred me awake. Reaching over to the nightstand, I turned on the lamp and, pushing back the covers, sat on the edge of the bed. Gazing around the room, my eyes slowly came into focus. Then I saw him, my father standing next to the bed. My eyes filled with salty tears, "Papa? Oh, my God, is that really you?"

He didn't speak but sat beside me, wrapping me in a warm hug. Closing my eyes, memories of the safety of his strong arms came flooding back from my childhood. Then, as I opened my eyes and gazed up at him, he smiled.

After rocking me in his embrace for several minutes, he finally broke the silence. "Allie, my little bird, you need this rest. There is much work to do as you have embarked on a quest that has put you and those you love in great danger. Know this; you will not fail them. I am here with you and your ancestors; we have guided you thus far. Please, my little bird, continue to listen to the messages you are receiving. If you do, you will have all the warriors of the ages with you, and you will not fail. You are about to embark on a course that will take you to your last battle in this war against your archenemy."

Standing, he turned, helped me lay down, and tucked me in snugly. "Now rest, my little warrior. You have a long road ahead of you."

"But, Papa—"

Gently resting his hand over my eyes, he nodded. "Rest, my dear. I am always with you."

Unable to fight it any longer, a heavy but peaceful feeling swept over me and carried me off to a night of deep and restful sleep.

Chapter 37

The next morning, I was sleeping so soundly that I almost didn't hear the wake-up call from the desk. Reaching over, I picked up the phone.

"Good morning, Ms. Callahan. This is your wake-up call. I hope you slept well last night."

Leaning up on one elbow at the edge of the bed, pushing my hair back from my face, I cleared my throat. "Thank you, and yes, I slept extraordinarily well. In fact, I think it was the best night's sleep I have gotten in days."

"I'm certainly glad to hear that. Breakfast is being served if you care to join us downstairs."

"Thank you, I think I will."

No sooner than I hung up the phone, picked up my bag, and headed to the bathroom, the phone rang a second time.

Picking it up, I cheerfully spoke into the phone. "Good morning. I already received my wake-up call, but thank you."

An unanticipated, deep, menacing, and all-too-familiar voice came from the receiver. "That's great! I'm delighted to hear that because soon you will need all the rest and strength you can get."

"Makya?"

"Why did you get so much sleep that you let your guard down? Especially after our little visit last night. I thought it might serve to motivate you."

"Makya, don't you ever learn? I will never let you call the shots. You can believe me when I say I never let my guard down. I am on your tail, just in case you haven't noticed!"

"Honestly, I haven't been really concerned enough to notice. I knew I didn't need to be. I was sure that you couldn't be far behind. Your precious friend, Claudia, is my guarantee for that."

"Let me talk to her."

"No, I don't think so. You'll just have to wait until you catch up with us."

"Makya, I'm warning you, if you harm one hair on her head—"

"You'll what?"

"I'll bring the wrath of all my ancestors down on you!"

"Well, you have to catch up with me first. Oh yes, and when you do, I think you owe me a basket of berries and herbs that are many years late! I'm going to make delivering them easy for you. I'm heading to South Carolina, and I'll be waiting for you in Murrells Inlet."

As I hung up the phone, I remembered Claudia's words of wisdom just before we left on this quest. She reminded me how brilliant Makya was and knew that he would try to rattle me by making me angry, to make me careless. She was right. Claudia also reminded me that Makya needed to face justice, and I might not be the one to serve it, but I could certainly bring him in to face it. I needed to stop and think things through. For now, time was on my side.

Closing my eyes, I took a deep breath and heard Grandfather's voice. *"Allie, fly with the wisdom of the eagle, your spirit animal. Soar above and be slow and steady on the hunt. Always have patients on the hunt. You never want your prey to see you coming or suffer. No fast moves until you are sure, then move in as swiftly as the breeze for the capture or the kill."*

"Allie! Hey, Allie! Earth to Allie!"

Opening my eyes, Emily was standing right in front of me.

"Allie, I think it's time to get a quick bite to eat and get on the road."

"I don't know if I want to take the time to eat. Maybe I can grab a coffee and bagel at Dunkin's."

Placing her hand up in my face, she firmly announced, "No! No, that will never do. You need your strength, and Makya will still be waiting for you to get to South Carolina. That jerk isn't going anywhere. Now keep your wits about you and get something to eat. Keeping him waiting might just frustrate him enough to throw him off his game a little. You're in the driver's seat and, at least for now, have the upper hand."

"You're right. Well then, in that case, I think I'll take a shower, get dressed, load my car and then have breakfast before I check out."

As she disappeared through the wall, she laughed. "Well then, come on, get a move on! You don't want to miss breakfast."

After taking my time getting ready, I was sitting in the dining room within the hour. A young girl approached my table with a coffee pot in hand. "Good morning. My name is Maryanne. Would you like some tea or coffee?"

Rolling my eyes with a sigh of anticipation, I lifted the cup upside down in a saucer on the table and placed it back down, face up. "Coffee sounds terrific!"

"Would you like the egg strata we are serving this morning or something lighter to eat?"

"I'm famished, so the egg strata sound lovely."

"Sure thing. That comes with a muffin and fresh fruit. Will that be okay?"

"That's perfect!"

After eating, I returned to my room to get my bag and headed to the desk to check out. Marta greeted me. "Good morning, Miss Callahan. I hope you had a peaceful sleep last night, honey."

"Oh yes, I slept like a rock. I even had a hard time waking up this morning. I'm glad I asked for a wake-up call, or I would probably still be sleeping."

"I'm so happy to hear that. Are you checking out or extending your stay with us?"

"As much as I would like to stay a couple more days, I fear I need to get back on the road."

"Okay then, let me get your invoice. I'll be right back."

As she walked from the desk, Emily was behind me. "Allie, we have to get out of here."

As Marta handed me my bill, Emily kept at me. "Allie, Payne, Josh, Jake, and the investigation team have moved ahead of us. Makya contacted Payne and told him he was headed to Murrells Inlet and planned to meet you there. They may even find him before us. That's not good, is it?"

Pulling out my wallet, I tried to act nonchalant. "Thank you, Marta. You have a beautiful little Inn here. I think I will bring my fiancé here after we're married. We might just have to plan a little cross-country trip."

"Thank you, Ms. Callahan. We would love that. If you haven't chosen a venue, we would be delighted if you consider our Inn for a getaway wedding."

"You know what? That is not out of the question. I'll keep that in mind."

Turning, I headed out the door with Emily on my heels. "Allie, haven't you heard one thing I said? I'm worried. I just found Payne and his crew. They've already made it to Dentsville, South Carolina. That's on the other side of Columbia and only about three hours from Murrells Inlet. And as for Makya, he is already in Murrells Inlet, just waiting for either of you to show up."

Stepping outside, I moved to my car as quickly as possible. "Emily, I heard everything you said, but you know as well as anyone that I can't respond to you when other people are around."

As I opened the car door, I turned in Emily's direction. "I'm sorry, Emily, you're right, I have to get a move on, but I have to stop and get Brick first."

Chapter 38

Payne, Josh, Jake, and Carl were driving in the lead vehicle heading to Murrells Inlet when Payne's cell phone rang. Not recognizing the number, he turned to Jake. "Hey, pull over. I need to get this. Hello, Payne here."

The phone was silent.

"Hello, this is Payne."

Still no answer. Growing angry, he growled, "This is Payne! Makya, you son of a bitch, is that you?"

It was Allie, and she couldn't hold back any longer. With tears streaming down her face, her voice cracked. "Payne? It's me!"

"Allie? Oh, my God, where are you? We drove halfway across the country, looking everywhere for you and Claudia."

She couldn't find her voice, and after another few seconds of silence, Payne panicked. "Allie, are you still there? Allie, talk to me."

Grabbing the phone out of Payne's hands, Josh desperately cried out, "Allie, honey, are you all right? Where are you?"

Allie choked out, "Josh, honey, it's so good to hear your voice. I love you!"

"I love you, too, Allie, but you need to tell me where you are. This is just crazy!"

"Josh, just listen! I can't tell you where I am, but please, for the sake of everyone with you, talk to them and turn them away from Murrells Inlet! Please don't go there. It's too dangerous!"

"Allie, come on, it would take an army to keep us from going. Makya has contacted Payne and told him he was meeting you there, and if we ever wanted to see you again, we had better be there as well!"

"Josh, honey, please listen to me! It's a trap. I can't explain everything now, but Claudia and I are going to end this once and for all."

"Claudia? Do you think that you and Claudia can stop this maniac? Honey, be reasonable."

"Look, Josh, I beg you, please don't meet Makya! Something terrible will happen if you do. I can feel it in every inch of my being. Please, I'm begging you! I have to go now. I love you."

Josh slammed the phone down on the seat and pounded the steering wheel. "Damn it, why can't she just trust us? She is going to get herself killed."

Jake reached up from the back seat, putting his hand on Josh's shoulder. "What the hell did she say?"

"She was warning us not to go to meet Makya. She thinks it's a trap."

Payne picked up the phone to check the caller ID. "Shit, the number she called from didn't come up. I'm sure she's using a burner phone. Even if we knew she would call and were ready to trace it, she's on the move, and it would be difficult."

Jake took a deep breath and groaned. "Payne, if that was a burner phone, she knows she took a chance opening communication with us and will probably destroy it, if she hasn't already."

Opening the car door, Payne got out. "You guys stay here. I'll go back to the other vehicle and tell everyone that Allie made contact. I'll be right back."

When Payne approached the van, Carl was in the driver's seat and already had his window rolled down. "Hey, Payne, what's up?"

"Allie just contacted us. She called me on my cell to stop us from meeting Makya."

"What? You have to be kidding, right?"

"No, unfortunately, I'm dead serious. Allie was trying to say it is too dangerous for us to meet Makya and that we are being lured into a trap."

"Well, one thing is for certain, now that we know about his plan, we're no longer walking blindly into that trap."

Chapter 39

After speaking with Payne and Josh, I destroyed the burner phone and went to Little's Playhouse Kennel to pick up Brick. I knew one thing for certain: Payne and Josh would not listen to me. They were going to meet with Makya, no matter what I said to them. I was on the road at nine o'clock and arrived in Murrell's Inlet by five that afternoon.

Pulling over at a gas station, I got out of the car, opened the trunk, and gazed down at my small arsenal of weapons and gear. Blowing out a puff of air, I chuckled as I took an inventory of what I had to work with. It wasn't lost on me that my arsenal was small, but I realized that the number of weapons I carried wasn't the important thing. I knew it was crucial to have the right weapons for the job. I had the crossbow, or latch, as they call it in Scotland, according to Liz. I had six shafts in a shoulder bag. In my handbag, I had my pistol and several rounds of ammunition. Unzipping the duffle bag, I dumped its contents on the trunk floor. Among the clothes, I found the six arrowheads and the belt and belt buckle I had brought from my ancestral box.

Unzipping the bag's front pocket, I pulled out the other stun guns and three burner phones Claudia and I purchased at Walmart in the Ozarks. Choosing one phone randomly, I turned it on and activated it.

I grabbed a protein bar and then, pulling the trunk lid down just enough to see over it, I looked through the car's back window. Brick's head was resting on the back seat, staring at me with those big brown eyes. "Are you hungry, boy?"

Lifting his head, he whined.

"Okay, Brick, give me a minute." As I lifted the trunk again, I grabbed his trail pack, pulled out one of the dog food pouches, poured some into his bowl, and gave it to him in the back seat. "Here you go, boy. Bon appétite!

Looking down at the bowl and then up at me, I could almost read his mind. He didn't want any part of what was in that bowl. I couldn't help but smile. "I'm sorry, Brick, that's the best I can do for now."

Climbing back into the driver's seat, I tore open the wrapper on my protein bar and took a bite. Looking up at Brick in the rearview mirror, I rolled my eyes. "I know, I know, boy! I'll tell you what, when I find a place for dinner, I promise to get you the biggest and juiciest steak I can find!"

A voice rang out from the passenger seat. "Hey, I wish you would stop talking about food all the time. That is one of the things I miss most of all, now that I'm on the other side."

Laughing, I almost spat out a piece of my protein bar. Wiping the crumb that had slipped out over my lips, I turned. "You sure do know how to make an entrance."

"I do, don't I? Hey, you spent some time at the in-between, didn't you?"

"The in-between?"

"Yeah, that place between your world and mine. You shouldn't do that, you know. It's just a couple of breaths away from where I am."

"Oh, you mean in suspended animation? That's something I learned to do many years ago."

"Well, you shouldn't be doing that anymore."

"I didn't go there by choice. Makya summoned me there. He actually learned that trick from me several lives ago. It was a safe place for me to confront him where he couldn't do me any physical harm."

"Well, there is a storm brewing, and it's beginning there in that space."

"I know."

"Yeah, but did you know that Makya has made arrangements for Payne to meet with him at a place called Drunken Jacks this evening?"

"You know I didn't, right?"

"Well, you do now, and Payne has agreed to meet him there alone at eight o'clock."

"Shit, you have got to be kidding me. Emily, I called Payne, told him he was in danger, and begged him not to go to Murrells Inlet. I knew I couldn't stop him from showing up there, but after my warning, I never dreamed he would meet Makya alone. What's worse is that everyone in the group would even consider letting him go on his own."

"Oh, they're not letting him do anything. They don't even know about it."

"Do you know where they're staying?"

"Yes, of course, I do!"

"Well, spill it then!"

"They're staying at a place called the Inlet Sports Lodge."

"I guess it looks like I need to find a pet-friendly place to stay myself and get checked in. I think I'll try a place like The Hampton Inn. They usually allow pets. I will need to get to that restaurant early and see if I can plant myself in an inconspicuous place where Payne won't see me when he arrives."

Looking in the rearview mirror, I started the car. "Do you think you can keep an eye on Payne and let me know when he heads out to meet Makya?"

When she didn't respond, I looked over to see she was already gone. "Geeze, Brick, you would think she would at least say goodbye, wouldn't you?"

Chapter 40

After checking in to my hotel, I got Brick settled in and paid a visit to the Inlet Sports Lodge. The plan was to visit and just stroll around to get a look at the place. Maybe I could get a quick peek at Josh from a distance.

My best-made plan got debunked when I stepped into the expansive lobby of the lodge, and a kind and polite gentleman greeted me at the desk. "Good evening. How can I help you?"

Whoops! I knew at that moment I hadn't quite thought the whole thing through. I had to think quickly!

"Good evening. I was in the area and thought I would come in to get some information about your beautiful establishment."

Handing me a brochure, he stepped out from behind the desk. "Why, thank you! Are you by chance planning a wedding or a small conference in the future?"

Trying not to stumble over my words and sound legitimate, I reached out to shake his hand and took a deep breath before answering. "Well, to be honest, I am planning a wedding, but I'm from Maine. I am, however, considering a destination wedding. I was in the area, and my friend, Emily, told me how much she liked it here. She and I have a mutual friend who stayed here a while ago and highly recommended it. Do you think I could just take a look around?"

"Certainly. That would be fine. Please let me know if you have any questions."

Stepping to the far end of the lobby, I pulled my burner phone from my bag. Lifting it to my ear, I began speaking into the receiver to look like I had received a call. "Hello, Emily. Are you in the area?"

Popping up in front of me with her smirky little expression, she boasted, "Now that's good thinking! You can talk to me, and no one will be the wiser. No one will ever know I am standing right here in the room talking to you."

"That's right, I'm here at the Lodge. It's every bit as beautiful as you said it would be. I thought I would take a walk around the grounds to see it all and then go for dinner. Do you have any other news for me?"

"Boy, Allie, you really are good at this!"

"Well, do you?"

"Yes, you should step into the restroom because Payne and his crew are about to enter the lobby from outside."

"Thank you. I'll see you there then."

I stepped into the ladies' room to continue the conversation with Emily. Popping in behind me, she scolded, "What were you thinking, coming here and standing out in the lobby for the whole world to see you? That really wasn't one of your better ideas."

"I know. I was just hoping I would get a chance to see Josh."

"Well, did you think there would be an equal chance that he or someone with Payne might have seen you? Anyway, I overheard them talking about going to Drunken Jacks for dinner with Payne, so I'm not sure how he will manage to meet Makya without any of them finding out."

"I'm not sure either, but if I know Payne, he'll figure it out. I'm going to head over there now. I need to get there early and find a table as far from the entrance as possible in hopes of staying out of eyeshot of Payne."

I waited ten minutes and then exited the ladies' room. There was no sign of Payne or the rest of his team. Moving quickly out the door to my car, I headed over to Drunken Jacks. A young hostess greeted me at the entrance. "Hi, I'm Kelly. Is there someone joining you this evening, or are you dining solo tonight?"

"It will only be me tonight. Could I possibly have a table back on the other side against the wall?"

"Sure, follow me."

Sitting in the perfect location, with a view of every part of the restaurant, it was seven-thirty, and I was feeling the storm building. I knew the first actual battle of this war with Makya was looming over me.

Promptly at eight o'clock, Payne, Jake, Josh, and the rest of the team walked in. They must have called ahead because the waitress took them to a large table set for seven. I raised my menu, covering my face until they were all seated, and ordered drinks. I wanted to run into Josh's arms and beg him to take me home, but I was too deep into this now to turn back.

That dreadful, looming feeling continued to crowd in on me. Something was coming, and I knew there was no way to avoid it.

After everyone at the table ordered their food, Payne got up. He handed Jake his credit card, left the table, and headed out the door.

"This is it. He's going to meet Makya. He just told

everyone he was not feeling well and would take an Uber back to the lodge. Allie, you have to get out of here and follow him."

Heeding Emily's warning, I got up, threw a fifty-dollar bill under the plate on my table, and moved for the door to follow Payne. Rushing out to the parking lot, there was no sign of him. Where the hell was he? He couldn't have gotten an Uber that fast.

"Allie, take the path that leads to the marsh. Payne's headed to the marsh."

"What path? Emily, what path?"

"He's at the marsh, behind Drunken Jacks!"

Moving as fast as my legs would carry me, I ran behind the restaurant. When I got there, I paused, scanning the area. It was dusk and getting difficult to see clearly. Then, I saw what looked like someone laying on the ground in the distance. I began running, slipping over the wet ground several times to find my worst fears had come to fruition. There he was, Payne, laying on the ground, bleeding from his neck.

Kneeling, I covered his throat with my hand. " Oh, my God, Payne, you're hit."

Choking on his blood, he spat out the words, "Allie, get out!" His blood splattered on my face. "Traps for you—get—." His head turned sideways on the wet, muddy ground.

Holding one hand over his throat, I pulled out my burner phone and dialed Josh's number.

He answered on the second ring. "Josh, oh, my God, Josh! It's Payne. He's been shot!"

"Allie, is that you?"

I was having difficulty speaking as I tried desperately to hold back the bleeding from Payne's neck.

Allie? Is that you? I'm having trouble hearing you."

"Yes, it's me! It's Payne. He's been shot! We're out behind Drunken Jacks at the marsh!"

The muzzle of a gun pressed against my neck. "Okay, Allie, give it up. He's gone. Get up and get a move on. Move it! Now! You better hope we get out of here before the others find us, or I might just have to take out someone else in your life."

Raising my hands in surrender, I got up and faced him.

"Don't try anything, Allie, or I promise you'll live to regret it. Now slowly, throw down that phone, and let's go to your car."

"If we do, we'll run right into Josh. I just called him, and I'm sure he is already on his way from the restaurant."

"Well then, I guess we'll have to go around the other side of the building. I mean it, Allie. Drop the phone and get moving. I will cut down anyone who gets in our way."

We ran across the marsh and around the other side of Drunken Jacks, avoiding the crowd moving toward Payne's body.

As we got to the edge of the parking lot, Makya grabbed my shoulder. "Stop right here! Where's your car?"

"It's that red Mustang in the last row near the exit."

"Nice ride, Allie. Now slowly give me your bag."

Taking the bag from me, he handed me a pair of handcuffs. "Attach one side of these to your right wrist."

Hesitating, I knew if he got me into them, it would go a long way in rendering me helpless.

"Put them on Allie! I'm not going to tell you again."

As I slid one side of the cuffs on my wrist, he smirked. "Put them on tightly. If you don't, I will do it for you myself, and believe me, if I do it... Well, let's just say if you don't want to lose your hand, you will put them on tightly enough to satisfy me."

After securing one side of the cuffs to my right hand, Makya checked it. "Smart move, Allie. Now you're getting it. You need to listen to me from now on or believe me, I will systematically take out everyone you care about."

Reaching down into my bag, he pulled out the keys to the car. "Well, is this all you're carrying? Mace on your key chain? Or is this pepper spray?" He laughed. "I guess you don't need any other weapons with the number of gifts you have. The trouble is, I still choose to carry guns and knives. I don't only rely on my gifts. Now turn around, hands behind your back."

Securing the other side of the cuffs to my left hand, he pushed his body against my back, hiding the handcuffs. Pressing his gun into my side, he looked around. "Okay, Allie, slow and steady. Let's get to the car, and you get in the passenger seat. No funny business or I'll cut you down where you stand. You know nothing is saying I can't wait another lifetime to join forces with you. I mean, I've waited this long. What's one more lifetime?"

We made our way to the car and got in. When Makya sat in the driver's seat, he rummaged through my bag again, pulling out my hotel key. Well, I guess this is where we're headed next. I'm sure you kept it a well-guarded secret, trying to protect your friends. Isn't it interesting that the things you did to keep your friends safe from me are now the very things that will keep me safe from them?"

"Makya, where is Claudia? What have you done with her? Is she alive?"

"Wow, slow down, Allie. First, I don't know if she is alive, and I definitely don't know where she is now. That little bitch somehow slipped out of my grasp and escaped. If I ever see her again, she will pay for that."

"I know I warned you I would finish you if you laid a hand on Claudia. I also know that no matter where she is now, you beat and hurt her before she escaped. So, I'm going on the record in saying this is a warning about your fate, Makya. I promise you that you will pay for what you did to Claudia and Payne."

"Well, since you are already sure you will be able to finish me, whatever that means, I guess it doesn't matter what I do to you or those you care about, so let me make this as clear as possible."

Aiming the gun, I thought he might shoot me, but instead, he struck me so hard on the side of my face that I saw stars.

"Is that clear enough for you?"

Chapter 41

As we walked into my hotel room, I struggled to stay conscious. Brick greeted us at the door and began circling me, sensing something was wrong.

Makya waved the gun at the other side of the room. "You take the bed farthest from the door and bring your mutt with you."

Brick raised his lips, showed his teeth, and let out a low, guttural growl.

"Unless you want me to put a bullet in that dog's head, you had better shut him up." He looked at the door to the adjoining room. "Wait, do you have the adjoining room as well?"

"No, but—"

"Well then, a bullet in the mutt's head it is." He aimed his gun at Brick.

"No, don't!" Looking at him with pleading eyes would never do the trick, empathy was not his forte. "I'll call the front desk and book that room!"

"Then do it!"

"How can I? My hands are behind my back."

Reluctantly, Makya, with his eyes and gun aimed on Brick, he moved over to the phone on the nightstand next to the bed, picked it up, dialed the front desk, and held it to my ear.

"This is Allie Callahan. I'd like to book the room next door to my room, please."

"Sure, Ms. Callahan. I believe it is available. I can unlock that door from here and you'll have full access to it. Is there anything else I can do for you, Ms. Callahan?"

"No, that's it. Thanks!"

Makya hung up the phone and turned his attention to the door when he heard it automatically unlock.

Makya opened the door to the second room. "Well, either you make him go in there, or I will. If I do it, you won't like how I manage to get him in there."

Walking through the door, I called Brick. I was sure he sensed something was wrong, as he reluctantly followed me into the room, where I led him over to one of the beds, and gave the command. "Lay down, Brick. Stay, boy."

When I joined Makya back in the other room, he closed the door behind me. Moving directly to the bed furthest from the door as he had instructed, I turned to find Makya standing so close that I could feel his hot breath on my face. Wrapping his arm around my waist, he pulled me into him and whispered, "Do you remember, Allie?"

Nausea rose in my gut, causing me to swallow bile. I wasn't sure if it was from getting clocked with his gun or because being this close to him revolted me! Letting out a breath of disgust, I groaned. "Remember what?"

"Do you remember the last time you and I were this close?"

Not responding to him, I just stood there, appearing still on the exterior as my insides trembled and the memories of him attacking me in my office whirled around in my head. He was so close now; his lips were almost brushing across mine.

"What? Nothing to say? Cat's got your tongue?"

Remaining quiet, I turned my head to avoid being within range for him to press his lips against mine.

Tightening his grip around my waist, he pressed his entire body against me. Stumbling back, the back of my legs grazed the bed. Then, pressing his lips against my ear, he whispered with a deep threatening tone, "I refuse to believe you've forgotten the night I surprised you in your office! I had entirely different plans for that evening, but you had to go and spoil it all, didn't you?"

I swallowed the vomit in my mouth.

"That infamous night you escaped from me through the office window? You remember? I know you do!"

Unable to contain my rage for another second, I leaned back, turned my head to face him, and head-butted him so hard across the face that his nose snapped.

Recoiling from me, he spat the dripping blood from his lips. "Well, there's the Allie we all know and love! Is that the best you've got, you arrogant bitch?"

Shoving me backward on the bed, he spat his blood out on the floor and stood over me. "It looks like I will be doing some...How did they put it in our previous lives? Some taming of the shrew?"

With great disdain, I growled back at him. "I don't know what your plans are, Makya, but if you haven't noticed, I'm not your obedient little squaw. I never was, and that's what always pissed you off. I don't know how you could ever believe I would help or join forces with you in any lifetime!"

"Well, I think it's safe to say that you can be persuaded! You have too much compassion for those in your life to let them suffer. Look, I was merciful with Payne. Let's just say the rest of your loved ones won't be so lucky. The more you resist, the more I will take those you care about most, one by one. Each time, their demise will be more and more sinister. Chew on that for the night, and we'll revisit this in the morning."

Turning, he moved away from me. "I think I will go after my things and get a bite to eat. Funny little coincidence, I won't even need to drive. I've been staying in a place that is within walking distance."

Pulling the handcuffs key from his pocket and demanding that I move up on the bed. "Lucky for me, they have a bed rail on the headboard."

After he secured the handcuffs around the bedpost, I rolled my eyes. "Do you really think this will keep me from getting free?"

Taking a tissue from a box on the nightstand, he wiped blood from his nose and then brazenly walked over to the desk in the corner of the room, dropping the keys there. Then, turning to me, he boasted, "Oh no, I'm not that naïve."

Pulling a syringe from his back pocket, he held it up, tapped it twice, and, removing the cover over the needle, he winked at me. "I have this, a special little cocktail I brought just for you. I think it should restrain you for quite a while."

Closing my eyes, I tried to calm myself. "I'm warning you, Makya, don't you come near me with that thing!"

He coughed. "Shit, Allie, I think you broke my nose!"

"I'll break more than that if you come near me with that needle."

"Look, Allie, we can do this the easy way, with this needle,

197

or the hard way, with a dart gun. It's your choice."

"I'm not letting you anywhere near me with that."

"Okay then, dart gun it is."

He pulled out a dart, loaded it, and then it was lights out for me.

Chapter 42

Makya pulled the dart from Allie's neck. Peering down at her, pleasure drenched his voice. "It was so much more enjoyable putting you out the hard way, you stuck-up bitch. You always have thought you were better than me, but you know what they say, he who laughs last?"

Moving to the bathroom, Makya picked up a leather pack in which he kept the darts and syringes, unfolded it, and slid the dart back into its sleeve.

Looking up in the bathroom mirror, he cursed. "Son of a bitch, what a mess she's made of my nose." Grabbing a facecloth hanging on the wall next to the sink, he wet it and washed the blood from his face.

As he leaned forward to get a closer look in the mirror, he groaned. "I am definitely going to need some ice for this!"

As luck would have it, the ice machine was in the hall, just a few doors down. Taking the ice bucket from the room, he retrieved some ice, brought it back, and, sitting at the desk, held some of it on his face for ten minutes.

Growing anxious to learn about what was happening back at Drunken Jacks, Makya moved from the desk, stood over Allie's bed, reached down, and began shaking her. "Hey there,

Sleeping Beauty, can you hear me?"

She didn't respond.

"I think it's safe to say that dart should keep you contained for a while. I'm going to get my things, a bite to eat, and, of course, check how much chaos I managed to stir up at Drunken Jacks this evening! I'm sure the heat will be rising on me now, so when I get back, we'll be moving out of here and heading back to Maine."

Picking up his wallet and the hotel key, Makya headed out the door. As he left, he turned and placed the do-no-disturb sign on the doorknob. "There, that should keep everyone away from the room."

Ten minutes later, Brick was whining at the door in the adjoining room when it swung open. "Okay, boy, where is she?"

Brick moved to the bed, jumped up, and sat beside Allie.

"Okay, boy, give me a minute."

Digging through Allie's backpack, they found the car keys and Brick's leash.

"Brick, come."

He wouldn't budge.

"Brick, you have to move. We don't have much time."

Snapping the leash to his collar, they dragged him off the bed. "Come on, Brick, I need you to take me to the car that belongs to this key."

When they got to the parking lot, Brick went directly to the red Mustang. "Wow, where did she get this fine automobile?"

Going through the car proved fruitless, but they hit the jackpot in the trunk. Gathering everything there and placing it into an empty backpack they found in the backseat, they called out to Brick. "Okay, buddy, let's go and get Allie."

As they returned to the room, they both sat on the bed next to Allie. "Okay, Brick, this is it! I'm getting better at this, but you better hold on to your collar 'cause here we go!"

Chapter 43

Still semi-conscious and groggy, someone rolled me over. "Allie. Hey, Allie."

My head was pounding. I opened my eyes, but I couldn't focus.

"Allie, for crying out loud, Allie, wake the hell up!"

As my eyes focused and I gazed up. I thought I was dreaming that I was laying on a forest floor, with the sun shining through a canopy of trees above me.

Without warning, someone forcibly pushed me up into a sitting position. Looking over to the left, I thought I saw Claudia. My mouth was as dry as cotton, as I swallowed. "This is some amazing shit Makya shot me with. I think I'm dreaming of being in heaven with Claudia."

Abruptly stunned by a slap across the face, I knew this couldn't be heaven.

"Wake up, Allie. We don't have time for this. You're not sleeping or tripping, you idiot. It's really me. This is not heaven, and we have to get the hell out of here."

"What? Claudia? Oh, my gosh, Claudia." Reaching out, I grabbed her and squeezed her as tight as possible. Leaning back, I touched her face. "Shit, it's really you! You're really here!"

Then it hit me. Pushing her away, I pursed and rolled my lips from side to side. "Girl, you have a lot of explaining to do! Where the hell have you been?"

"You're right. I promise I'll explain everything, but right now, I'm going to take you somewhere safe until you have your wits about you."

Picking up the duffle bag, Claudia dragged me to my feet and called out, "Brick, come!"

Once I was on my feet and moving, and my eyes began to focus, standing about ten feet away was my infamous horse, Noya. Claudia's voice became more urgent as she dragged me over to him. "Come on, Al, let me give you a leg up."

Climbing on her horse, she grabbed the end of the rope that hung around Noya's neck. "Okay, Al, hang on, we have to move. I know you're still groggy, but you have to sit tight. Hang on to his main if you need to.

She led me down a small hill and into a river. Staying at the river's edge to avoid its strong current, we made our way upstream about a mile. Stopping, she gazed around. "I think this will be okay."

"Okay for what?"

"Okay, for us to stop and rest. At least long enough for you to get your legs back under you and your mind cleared from whatever it was that Makya shot into your bloodstream."

Dismounting, she stepped over to Noya to help me down. "Come on, there's a clearing just beyond the trees. We can hang our wet close in the sun there and still have the protection of the woods to hide in."

Looking down, my head still woozy, I grinned as I saw

our reflections in the stream. "Hey, Claudia, look there. Those are the identical versions of us that Grandfather showed us in the windowpane."

Then, still feeling a bit weak, my knees went out from under me, landing me face-down in the river.

Grabbing me by the back of my shirt, Claudia pulled me up, and, taking my arm, she couldn't help but laugh. "Allie, I think you're still a little buzzed, but we still need to keep moving. We have to cut a path through these thick woods wide enough for the horses to get through."

Using a crude ax of some type, Claudia began cutting back the trees and thickets, making a path for us to the clearing.

"Hey, Claudia, where did you get that? How long have you been here? I was so worried about you."

Shaking her head, Claudia turned to me and laughed. "Let's get to the clearing, get settled in, and get you sobered up. Then I'll explain everything. We have some work to do before sundown."

"Work? Like what kind of work?"

"Allie!"

"I know, I know, less talking and more walking!"

"That's right, we have to get our wet clothing hung before we lose the sunlight. And we definitely need to gather enough firewood to protect us from the cold and any predators throughout the night. Come on, get a move on."

Claudia stopped and threw me some dry clothes as we got to the clearing. "Here, give me your clothes and put on this dress and moccasins. They're more appropriate for the time we're in now. You can't go running around in clothes from another century!"

Giggling, I pulled my clothes off over my head and began

mumbling under my breath. "Sure thing, boss. Aye, Aye, captain, okey-dokey, Smokey."

"I heard that, Allie!"

Looking down, Brick was sitting at my feet, and my head started spinning as I squeaked out, "She heard that, boy. Did you hear—"

Then it was lights out again!

Waking up several hours later, I was laying beside a fire, with Brick's hot breath on my face. As I sat up, I vaguely remembered where I was, but still a little unsure about the details of how I got there."

Claudia was sitting on a rock next to the fire, stoking it with a long stick. "Welcome back, Allie."

"OMG, my head is pounding."

"I bet it is. You really tied one on. Well, with Makya's help, of course."

"How long have I been out?"

"I would say about seven hours. You really needed to sleep that one off. It's pretty clear that Makya's intention was to keep you sedated as long as possible. Keeping you like that… Let's just say that is probably the only way he felt confident he could keep the upper hand for a while."

Still not thinking clearly, my brain and mouth felt like someone stuffed cotton in them. Finally, I found my voice. Tears welled in my eyes. "Claudia, Payne is dead!"

"What? No!"

"Yes, he's dead. Makya shot him."

"Are you sure? How do you know?"

"Because I was there. I begged Payne not to meet Makya, but he went anyway, and he went alone. That's the only way Makya would agree to meet with him. I thought it was a trap for Payne, but with his dying breath, Payne said it was a trap for me. And to make it worse, it worked.

"Makya shot Payne in the neck. I tried to stop the bleeding by holding my hand over the wound, but he bled out right there in front of me. I called Josh because he was close by with the investigation team, but Makya put a gun to my neck and got me out of there before Josh reached us."

"Allie, are you absolutely sure Payne is dead? Maybe he just passed out."

"No, he was gone. I just know it!"

Claudia stood up and began pacing. "That son of a bitch! We're going to get that bastard, and we're going to get him tomorrow. I'm done playing his games." Picking up the duffle bag, she began unzipping it. "I took these things from the trunk of the car you were driving. I see you have a crossbow and even some shafts for the arrowheads we took from the ancestral box."

"How about the belt and belt buckle? Did you get that?"

"I certainly did!"

"Well, I haven't figured out why we need that, but at least we have it. Now we just have to find Makya."

"That won't be a problem. I know exactly where we can find him."

"Where?"

"In the teepee, you and Calian, as we know him in this lifetime, share. It's right on the other side of this clearing. Do you remember when you told me about the morning you saw this version of me here? That morning when you left, you said that you had an argument with Calian and that you were going to pick berries and herbs. I tried to stop you, but you left and never came back. That day you escaped Calian in this lifetime. Allie, I've brought us back to that exact time.

"Tomorrow morning, he will wake up and be angry with you because you will not be laying with him in your dwelling. Then he will go off on his hunt. That's when we'll get him. We'll follow him this time when he leaves and confront him in the woods."

"But, Claudia, he won't be alone. He'll be with another hunter. Whoever that is could get caught in the crossfire."

"Well, we'll just have to see that whoever it is doesn't. It's a chance we have to take."

"Okay, I get it."

"Come on, Allie, we need to build another fire back in camp. You'll need to sleep there the rest of the night and confront him in the morning, just as you did before."

Chapter 44

The next day, I woke up next to the fire not far from the teepee I shared with Makya, or Calian, as they called him in this lifetime. Getting up from the fire, I moved closer to our dwelling, and just as before, Calian stepped out, grabbing me by the arm, pulling me into the teepee, and shoving me to the ground. Then, moving to the edge of the teepee, he grabbed the large round basket and shot it at me. Looking into his face, I saw those familiar eyes. Those dark brown eyes belonged to a man I knew all too well. Makya!

He spoke the exact angry words he had before. "You are a lazy dreamer. Why you insist on leaving our dwelling and choose to lay with the fire in place of me is a mystery. You need to do your gathering, and you are late in starting your day. I am off to hunt. You will obey me and begin behaving like a squaw worthy of me."

Then, just as I remembered, I heard footsteps outside as someone approached. "Calian, are you coming? We are late; the morning is half over."

Just as I had done before, I got up on my knees. Calian glared down at me, striking out in my direction, not laying a hand on me. And again, as before, his powers knocked me back to the ground. This time I knew better and did not raise my hand, but sat back, keeping my anger in check.

Then I heard him repeat the words I was most dreading. "That's right, you know better than to challenge me. I will strike you down every time. Your powers are no match for mine!"

Then, just as I remembered, he pushed through the opening in the structure and paused without turning to me. "Do not return this afternoon unless you have filled that basket with berries and some healing herbs. You must learn your place and mind your responsibilities. Do not make me the laughingstock of this tribe one more time!"

Laying on the ground, I didn't budge until I heard him riding off on his horse.

Once I was sure he was gone, I picked up the basket and went out in search of Claudia. She was waiting for me at the edge of the clearing with Brick and our ponies.

As I approached her, she pulled the bag that held the shafts from the duffel. "I took the liberty of mounting the arrowheads on the shafts while you were sleeping last night."

As I threw it over my shoulder, she pulled out the crossbow strung on the belt and belt buckle so I could carry it on my shoulder. "And here, in case we should get separated. You can't do much with those arrows if you have nothing to shoot them with."

"How about my gun, ammunition, and the mace?"

"Check, check, and check. I also have our protein bars and Brick's trail pack in the duffle."

"Well, it looks like we have all we planned to bring."

As we mounted our horses, Claudia looked over at me. "Not that it matters, but do you remember your name in this lifetime?"

"It was Winona, right?"

Yes, and mine was Enola. Also, just to let you know, the other hunter, with Calian, is Hania. Or as we know him, in our true time, Jake."

"Okay then, Enola, let's get this done. I know Makya has hunted several times in a valley just a few miles from here. He has told me that the buffalo are plentiful there. I think it's a good place to start."

Picking up Makya and Hania's trail just beyond the tree line before heading out of camp. as we suspected, they were heading for the valley. Following their trail, within the hour, we found ourselves in an eyeshot of where the herd was grazing. As we looked out over the plush grounds, there were buffalo as far as the eye could see.

"Allie, you weren't kidding when you said the buffalo were plentiful here. Aren't they amazing?"

"They are, but history has taught us that the white man will deplete the herd over the next several years, reducing their numbers, which will force our people to reservations. Some will avoid that in the short term by moving west, forming what has become known as The Trail of Tears. They will settle in the Midwest, avoiding their fate temporarily, but ultimately they will succumb to it. In our true time, that is in the past. Looking forward, we need to remember those lessons and make sure those things never happen again. Come on, follow me."

Backtracking, we tied our horses in the trees and walked back to where the buffalo were. "I don't understand. Where are Makya and Hania? They should have been here before us?"

"No, about a mile back, their tracks went north. They will come into the valley from there. Makya knows if they cause a stampede, it will drive the herd south and not back toward the camp. He has bragged to me many times about his hunting techniques. Ironically, in this case, it will prove to be helpful to us as we hunt him. We need to just sit in the trees and watch for them to come back this way, and then we can take him out."

Leaving Brick at the base of one of two trees about twenty feet apart, Claudia and I perched ourselves just high enough to remain out of sight from the ground but close enough to see each other.

It seemed like forever, but as grandfather always said, *"Little Bird, always remain quiet on the hunt, patient on the hunt, and don't let your prey see you coming."*

A few hours later, Claudia hand-signaled to me. They were coming, and she had spotted them.

Quietly, I climbed down to Brick at the base of the tree and awaited Claudia's signal. Taking the crossbow off my shoulder, I loaded an arrow. Makya's laughter came from a distance as they grew even closer. Then I saw them. Each had their packhorse in tow, with their game strung and secured.

Brick's lip quivered. I gave him the hand signal for out, so he would stand down. As they drew closer, a branch broke under Claudia's feet, sending an echoing sound across the area. Hania raised his hand to Makya. They stopped and went silent. Beads of sweat welled on my forehead as I stood and looked on. Finally, Makya burst out laughing. They heard nothing more, and must have concluded that it was just an animal or bird pushing off a branch.

Picking up my weapon, I aimed it at Makya. I wanted a direct hit to his heart. No suffering, just one blow, and he would be gone.

Grandfather's words pounded in my ears repeatedly. *"Quiet on the hunt, patient on the hunt, no suffering. Quiet on the hunt, patient on the hunt, no suffering."*

I took my shot. It was a direct hit. Makya flew off his mount, but Hania's horse reared and spooked, sending him flying into a tree. He bounced off and lay on the ground, unconscious.

Claudia climbed down and rushed over to Hania as I ran to Makya. I was right. It was a direct hit and he was dead instantly.

Rushing over to Claudia, I looked at Hania, her husband of this lifetime, and realized immediately he was in trouble. A tree branch had punctured his arm, severing an artery, and he was bleeding out. It was at that moment I knew the purpose of the belt and belt buckle. I wrapped it tightly around his arm to stop the bleeding.

Looking up at Claudia, I cried, "We need to get him back to the tribe. He needs to see the medicine man."

"What will we tell them? We will be accused of murdering Makya. The tribe will find us guilty, and we will never be able to return to our true time."

"Yes, we will. Hania never saw us. We can say we were collecting berries and herbs when we came across them. Makya was dead, and Hania was passed out. We found them and brought them back. That's all."

Hania started coming to, and we sat him up. Claudia cried and began nervously babbling. "Hania, are you okay? What happened to you? We need to get you back to camp. You have been hurt."

Helping him to his feet, we got him up on his horse. Looking up at him, I explained, "Our horses aren't far from here. We will take you and your horses with us to get ours and take you back to the camp. Do you think you can ride?"

He didn't speak, but nodded instead.

When we arrived back at the settlement, a crowd ran out and surrounded us, spewing questions and their concerns. "What happened? Is he all right? Where is Calian?"

They immediately took Hania down from his horse and carried him off to the tent of the medicine man. Claudia followed them, and taking Brick and the duffle bag full of our supplies, I went to the fire and waited for word of his condition.

I must have been sitting there for an hour when I looked up to find my great grandmother, Catori standing over me.

Seeing her overwhelmed me to tears. "Grandmother, I am so sorry!"

Sitting down next to me, she wrapped her arm around my shoulder, pulling me close to her in a hug. With the other hand, she passed me the belt and belt buckle. "My Little Bird, I believe this belongs to you. Do not despair. You have done what you needed to do. By ending Makya's life with one of those arrowheads, he will lose his powers for the rest of his future lives. But be warned, it may take some time for him to lose all of his abilities. Be very careful when you go back to deal with him in your true time. You and your friend must go back, while the part of your spirits that belong here will remain. There is still much work to do in the lives you are living now and the ones that are yet to come. Now it's time to gather your friend and go. Go to your true time. Keep listening to your ancestors and know that you still have many more to meet and learn from. I love you, Little Bird."

Taking Brick and our things, I got up and walked to the large tent of the medicine man. Standing at the entrance, I pulled open the slit in the teepee and looked at Claudia. "Could I speak with you for a second?"

Getting up, she stepped out, joining me.

I wiped a tear from her cheek. "How is he?"

"He's alive. He is in and out of consciousness, but still alive."

"Claudia, I just spoke with Grandmother Catori, and she said it is time for us to go."

"Allie, how can I leave him now?"

"Look, I understand, but I spoke to Grandmother. She said, even when we leave, the part of our spirit that belongs in this time will remain. You won't really be leaving him. What we need to do is to return to our true time and finish this work there. And we need to get back to Josh and Jake, right?"

"Yes, you're right."

Pulling my pendant out of my shirt, I smiled. "Do you have yours?"

"Yes, I do! And if you think it's okay, I would like to do the honors this time."

"Oh, I don't know about that. You are still pretty new at this."

"Come on, Allie. Where is your sense of adventure? Besides, I got you here. Didn't I?"

I took Brick's collar in my hand. "Well then, since you put it that way. Okay, but let's get a move on."

Claudia swinging her pendant caused me to panic.

"Wait, even though we have only been here a couple of days, we don't know how long we have actually been gone from our true time, so take us back to my hotel."

"Okay, the hotel it is."

Chapter 45

The next thing I knew, I was sitting in the red Mustang in the hotel parking lot. Adjusting the rearview mirror, I smiled at Brick and then turned to Claudia. "Looks like you did it. We're back safe and sound. Do you think you could reach in the back seat and grab one of the two burner phones we still have left and activate it? I think it's time to call Jake and Josh!"

"Gladly!"

Claudia reached back and pulled the duffle from the back seat, placing it on the floor at her feet. Unzipping the bag's front pocket, she pulled out the keys to the car. "I think you'll be needing these."

"Yes, I certainly will. Now let's get the guys on the cell. Claudia called Jake's phone. As it rang over and over, she turned to me. "Al, he's not answering. He's not picking up. It just keeps ringing."

"Are you sure you dialed the right number?"

"Allie, are you kidding me right now? Of course, I did, but I didn't leave a message. I wasn't sure if I should."

Claudia handed me the phone. "Here, try Josh."

Putting the phone on speaker, I dialed his number. It rang four times and then went to voicemail. "Hello, this is Josh Sullivan. Thanks for calling. Please leave your name, number, and the reason you'd like to chat, and I'll get back to you ASAP."

Without leaving a message, I hung up and looked down at the phone, and with relief, I turned to Claudia. "According to the date on this cell phone, we haven't lost any time. It's only been a few days since we left."

"Well, that's great, but where are Josh and Jake?"

"I don't know, but why don't we go to Inlet Sports Lodge, where they were staying, and see what we can find out?"

Putting the key into the ignition, I hesitated and turned to Claudia, rolling my eyes.

"Allie, what?"

I nodded toward the back seat.

"We have company, don't we?"

"Yep!"

Emily piped up. "Well, it's about time you got back. It's been a bit chaotic since you left for your little trek in time! Josh and Jake are worried sick! And to say Makya is pissed would be the understatement of the century!"

"Allie, what? What is she saying?"

"According to Emily, the good news is that Jake and Josh are safe. Worried sick, but safe. The bad news is that we have pissed Makya off beyond belief!"

Emily interrupted. "Do you mind if I ask you where you have been and what you have been up to? You both went totally off my radar."

Holding one finger up to Claudia, I winced. "Give me a second. I need to bring Emily up to speed."

Looking back at Emily in the rearview mirror, I puffed out, "It's kind of a long story, but to make it short, we went to a previous life to take Makya's powers from him."

"Really! Wow, he doesn't have the power to confront you anymore?"

"That's what we're hoping. Although it may take some time, his powers will dissipate slowly. He may not even notice it yet."

Claudia laughed. "Okay, you two, need I remind you? I still cannot hear both sides of this conversation, and Al, we still don't know where to find the guys."

Clearing my throat, I looked at Emily again in the rearview mirror. "Well?"

"Oh yeah, I can help with that. They're both at the morgue in Conway. Something to do with Payne's autopsy."

"Oh, my God! Thank you, Emily!"

Anxious to find the guys, I checked the phone's GPS. "We need to go to the coroner's office. Emily just said that Jake and Josh are there."

Claudia grabbed my arm. "Allie, wait, let's think this through. We still have some unfinished business. If we go to Josh and Jake now, they won't let us out of their sight again."

Huffing, I slumped back into my seat. "Shit, you're right!"

"Look, Al, I want to see them just as much as you do, but we can't go back now. We have one more burner phone. Maybe we can just leave them a message, letting them know we're all right, and then destroy the phone we use."

I picked up the burner phone and dialed Josh's number a second time. This time, he picked up on the second ring, and with urgency, he began, "Hello? Hello? Who is this?"

Covering the phone with my hand, I whispered, "Crap, he answered."

His anger grew. "Hello, is this you, Makya, you son-of-a-bitch? There is nowhere you can go! You can run to the furthest point of the Earth, and I will still find you, you coward. You're done, you hear me? You're done!"

My voice cracked. "Josh? Josh, it's me!"

The phone went silent.

"Josh, honey, it's me!"

"Allie? Allie, oh, my God! Allie?"

"Yes, it's me."

Panic rose in his voice. "Are you all right? Has Makya got you? Where the hell are you? Is Claudia with you?"

"Josh, please slow down and listen. I'm safe, and so is Claudia."

"Where are you? We'll come and get you! Honey, tell me where you are?"

"I can't do that."

"What does that mean? We've already lost—"

"I know. I know about Payne! I knew he was gone when I called you from behind the restaurant. When I was talking to you, Makya came up behind me, put a gun to my neck, and forced me out of there before you could reach us. I'm so sorry!"

"Allie, please, I'm begging you. Please tell me where you are."

"I can't, Josh. I'm so sorry, but I can't. You just have to trust me. I have to finish this. Then and only then will we be free to live our lives without fear."

"But. Allie—"

Hanging up before he could persuade me to change my mind, I slammed the phone down on the steering wheel, smashing the screen. "Claudia, I'm not sure if Josh will ever forgive me!"

"Of course, he will, but we have to finish this so we can get on with our lives. I think we need to set up some sort of trap for Makya. What's our next move?"

"We should do something he might think we would never do, like get another room at the Comfort Inn."

"I don't get it. How is that a trap?"

"It's the first place he'll check. Think about it, at first he'll consider that is the last place we'll go. Then, he'll think we already thought of that, just for that reason. He will think it's the perfect place for us to hide. Kind of reverse psychology. Then, just in case I'm wrong, we will make ourselves visible all over town before we retire for the evening."

"That's brilliant! Think about it, though. Do we really want to confront him at the hotel? I mean, Allie, it could get pretty messy, don't you think?"

"Good point. You're right. We'll need to lure him somewhere else. Maybe behind the restaurant where he killed Payne."

Chapter 46

We checked back into the Comfort Inn, showered, and began getting ready for our night on the town. Everything was eerily serene. You could say it was quiet enough for us to consider letting our guard down, but we knew better.

Claudia complained from the bathroom. "I guess these jeans and jersey will just have to do. It seems we packed a little light."

Dancing over to her, I straightened her necklace. "Come on, where's my friend who can put her groove on and have fun anywhere in any time or place, under any circumstances? After all, we packed for a lot of hiking, not a night on the town. Besides, it's the beach, and we're supposed to look like we're on vacation. That's perfect."

Leaving Brick in the room, we headed out and went to Drunken Jacks. As we stepped into the restaurant, the hostess, Kelly, who apparently remembered me, greeted us. "Well, hi there! I think we owe you a meal since the last time you were here. You left before we could get your food to the table. We were wondering if you were okay. We had a great deal of excitement out back that night."

"I'm fine. Thank you for your concern. I suddenly began feeling ill that night and had to return to my hotel."

"I'm certainly glad to hear that. Your waitress this evening will be Diane. Please follow me."

As she showed us to our seats, I turned, whispering to Claudia, "Apparently, all the circumstances of that evening made me a memorable guest."

"You think?"

Everything remained quiet for our entire meal. After we ate our entrees, Diane cleaned off our table. "Would you ladies like some dessert?"

I turned to Claudia with pleading eyes. "What do you think?"

"No, but maybe an after-dinner drink? A Bailey's, perhaps?"

"Ooh, that sounds like an even better idea. Make that two and the check when you have a minute."

Five minutes later, Diane brought us our Bailey's. Before placing the check on the table, she hesitated. "I just want to let you both know that your bill has been taken care of."

The hairs on the back of my neck stood straight up, and Claudia's face went as pale as her white jersey.

Seeing our shocked expressions, the smile left Diane's face. "I hope that's all right?"

Lifting my Bailey's to take a sip, I stuttered, "Oh, ah, no. Is the gentleman still here? I mean, yes, that's fine. That was very kind. We'd like to thank him."

"No, he paid his tab and has left. He has become one of our regulars for the past couple of weeks."

As Diane walked away, I shifted my gaze to the door. "What do you think, Claudia?"

"Excuse my language, but I think it's been too effing quiet all day."

"Claudia, you never use the eff word!"

"I know, but I think this situation deserves nothing less."

"Okay, before we leave this place, we need to consider our next move. We have to assume it was Makya who picked up our check."

"Al, of course, it was! Who else could it have been?"

"I'd like to believe it was some kind stranger, but we both know that's not likely. I have my pistol and mace in my purse. How about you?"

Sliding a large steak knife off the table and slipping it into her bag, she grinned nervously. "I have mace and one heavy-duty steak knife!" Then, Claudia's eyes got as large as the saucers on the table.

"Claudia, what's wrong?"

"Allie, look behind you! Can you see what I see? What the heck is going on?"

Before I even turned to look, I knew what was happening. Everything had gone still. There was no chatter, no dishes or glasses clanging, and the bartender was standing like a statue, as the alcohol he was pouring was suspended in mid-air.

"Claudia, we are suspended in time. Sort of between our world and the next, and I'm not doing this!"

"Al, I don't even know what *this* is. What the heck are you talking about?"

"We are not in our time or in a parallel time. We're suspended in what's called the in-between, or at least that's what Emily calls it."

"So, if you didn't do this, I guess it's a safe guess that we definitely know who paid for our dinner!"

"Claudia, I want you to listen to me very carefully. We are going to get up very slowly. I will face the door, and I want you to stand up and put your back to mine. Take out your knife and mace. We are going to walk out of here, back-to-back."

"Holy crap, Al, are you sure about this?"

"No, I'm not, but I don't want us to get trapped in this place if we can help it."

As we moved toward the restaurant entrance, the door was open, and a dark cloud was rolling into the building, covering the ceiling. "OMG, Claudia, there's a storm coming!"

As Claudia looked up, the clouds moved in over her head. "No offense, Allie, but this is really crazy! Is it actually going to rain in here?"

"No, Claudia, those are war clouds, not rain clouds."

Spinning around, she took one look at my face and understood. Allie, your face. It's the same face we saw in our reflections in the window. The one's grandfather showed us. Is this it? Are we really going to battle right now?"

"It's entirely possible. Makya must still have some of his powers because he has to be the one doing this. Come on, back-to-back, let's get out of here."

Moving through the door and outside, the air around us was calm and still, but as before, the dark billowing clouds rolled over our heads, lighting the sky with enormous bolts of lightning.

Stepping into the parking lot, I scanned the area. "Claudia, do you see him?"

"No, I don't. Where the hell is he?"

"If he's the one doing this, he must be close. Keep your eyes peeled."

Suddenly, I spotted him. "Claudia, no matter what, I need you to remain calm and keep your back to mine."

"Why? Do you see him?"

"Yes, I do, and he's headed our way!"

Walking over to us from across the street, Makya crowed. "Well, well, I can't believe you haven't run for the hills. I mean really, Allie, after Claudia saved you and all. Why would you hang around here, just waiting to be captured again?"

"Makya, is that what you think we're doing? Do you think we're just waiting for you to capture and hold us hostage until I submit to your will? What an overblown ego you have. After all this time, you haven't learned anything, have you?"

"Allie, I don't think your precious Payne will be able to swoop in and help you this time, will he?"

"I'm warning you, keep Payne's name out of this!"

"Oh, and what are you going to do about it?"

As the anger grew in me, I couldn't speak!

He began bellowing. "Come on, Allie, use your words! Tell me what you think you can do about it. Let me remind you again, *Payne is dead!*"

That was it. I lashed out with my tongue. "It could be the difference between your leaving this life in a mercifully swift manner or suffering a long and agonizing death! One way or the other, you're going down."

Claudia screamed. "Allie, this isn't you! Don't let him goat you into being like him!"

She was right, but I couldn't hold my rage back one second longer. "Why don't you take us out of this suspended time and fight like a real man?" Raising my hand, I continued to taunt him. "Come on, you coward! Do it or do I have to do it myself?"

The clouds began dissipating. His powers were failing, and his ability to keep us suspended in time was waning.

"Go ahead," Makya shouted. "Give it your best shot!"

As my anger grew, I raised my arm in Makyas direction and drew on my skill to levitate him. Lifting Makya twenty feet, Ithen released him, watching him slam down to the pavement.

Staggering to his feet, he laughed cynically. "Is that all you've got? You must be losing your touch, Allie. Come on, why don't you try that again?"

Claudia elbowed me. "What the hell are you doing? Don't let him do this?"

Ignoring her, I yelled, "No, I think it's your turn, Makya! Give it your best shot!"

Claudia stung me with her elbow again. "Allie, are you crazy?"

Makya's arrogance hadn't waned. "If you insist!"

Pulling back his arm, he swung it toward me with so much force that it took him to the ground. Confused, he got up and struck out again. Looking down at his arm, and then at me, his face became dark with disdain and hatred.

Turning to run, he cried, "You bitches, what have you done?"

The minute he took his first step, I reached out again, lifting him up and turning him to face my anger. "You have threatened me or anyone else for the last time, Makya. It's over!"

He started flailing in mid-air. "You just wait until our next lives. I will come back and finish you. I promise. Believe me, you will say I was merciful in this life. I will come back stronger and more powerful than ever."

The clouds had completely lifted as I raised my pistol. Moving closer to where he was suspended, I lowered him down on his feet where I could look him in the eye. "No, I don't think so, Makya. You see, I made sure that you could never gain those powers ever again?"

He spat on the ground and lunged at me, forcing me back and causing me to trip over Claudia's leg. "What the hell have you done?"

As he lunged toward Claudia, I took my shot, sending him to the ground.

Stunned, I called out to Claudia. "Are you okay?"

"Yes, but Makya's not."

Getting to my feet, I turned to see Makya laying on the ground, a shot to his head. As blood began streaming from his wound, activity on the street resumed—traffic and crowds. "Someone call the police!"

"Call an ambulance!"

"Ma'am, my name is William. Are you okay? I saw the whole thing!"

Suddenly, above all the commotion, two car doors slammed. "Please step back! Give us some space."

"Ma'am, please step back!"

I inhaled and let out a sigh of relief when I heard, "Oh, my God, Jake! It's Allie and Claudia!"

William stepped up and got between Josh and me. "Sir, I saw the whole thing. That man was harassing and shoving these women around. She was acting in self-defense. That guy shoved her to the ground and went after her friend before she shot him."

Detective Carl Johnson stepped up to William. "Sir, could I take your statement?"

"Certainly. I would love to help in any way I can!"

"Please follow me to my car, and we can make out a report."

Josh hugged me so tight I thought he might break one of my ribs. Stepping back, brushing the hair off my face, he closed his eyes and kissed me. "Allie, honey, I can't believe you're finally here, safe and sound! You have no idea how worried I've been!"

Caressing his face, I groaned. "Oh, I think I might have an idea. I think I know how it feels to think the person you love might be dead!"

Chapter 47

Two days later, we arrived at the Summit. As we got out of the car, Mom, Guile, and Ben, Claudia's father, were anxiously waiting in the doorway. The minute our feet hit the pavement; they came running out.

With tears streaming from her face, Mom wrapped her arms around me. "Oh, honey, we have all been so scared."

Stepping back, she ran her hand across my cheeks, wiping away my tears. "You're going to be okay now, honey! You're, by far, one of the bravest women I have ever known and definitely a chip off your old father's and grandfather's blocks."

"I love you, Mom! I am so glad to be home. I am truly sorry for all the worry we've caused everyone!"

With a grin, Mom tapped her index finger to her cheek. "Hmm, what was it I always said when you were younger, each time you got in trouble and scared me half to death?"

Pursing my lips in a half-smile, I shook my head and rolled my eyes. "You always said, 'I don't know if I want to hug you or punish you.' I think I'm a little old for punishment, don't you?"

"Honey, I'm so grateful that you and Claudia made it back to us safe and sound. Nothing but hugs and kisses will do! I hope you guys don't mind, but Guile, Ben, and I made some dinner for everyone. We have a ham in the oven with scallop potatoes. Would you care to join us in the penthouse for something to eat?"

We all started clamoring at once!

"Yes, we're starving!"

"Great, we don't have to cook. We probably don't have any food to make anyway!"

"Yes, yes, a home-cooked meal at last!"

After making our way up to the penthouse, we set the food on the table and sat down to eat. At first, no one spoke. I don't think anyone knew exactly what they should say.

Standing from my chair, I glanced around everyone at the table until my eyes locked on Josh. Somehow, I knew I had to clear the air and break this deafening silence. With some reservation, I found my voice. "Hey, everyone, um…"

Josh stood. "Allie?"

Finding strength in the safety of his eyes, the words came. "I think someone needs to just talk a little about the elephant in the room. I know Claudia and I have a lot to explain, but tonight, I would just love to sit here with my family and enjoy the luxury of not having to look over my shoulder every minute. I just want to feel like things are normal again, whatever that is.

Josh took my hands in his. "I second that."

Then, without skipping a beat, he turned to the table and declared, "Besides, I think we've got more important things to talk about. Don't we have an upcoming wedding to plan? I would much rather talk about that. All in favor?"

Everyone in the room exhaled and raised their hands as Jake leaned in to kiss Claudia and bellowed, "I think the ayes have it!"

Mom jumped up immediately. "Wait, I'll be right back!"

She returned to the room with a three-ring binder. "I hope you don't mind, Allie, but I continued working on your wedding while you were gone."

"That's great, Mom!"

That's all I had to say. Her excitement grew, the starting gate opened, and she was off.

"Really? You don't mind? I have so many suggestions! Of course, they're just suggestions, but I had to do something to keep my mind off things while you were gone. I had faith, though. I knew you would be back!"

Guile burst out laughing. "I can vouch for that! She kept looking at venues, catering companies, and florist options the whole time you were gone."

After finishing our meal, we cleared the table, and Guile served an after-dinner wine. Mom began showing us all the research she had done. We were genuinely content and having fun for the first time in a very long time.

About an hour later, Josh looked up at me. "Honey, I don't mean to be a party pooper, but you look beat. Maybe you can skip the station tomorrow, take a few days off, and get some rest. In fact, maybe you, Claudia, and your mom can work on these wedding plans."

"I am exhausted, but I really want to be with Brian for Payne's autopsy tomorrow."

Mom reached over, ran her hand over my cheek, and half-smiled. "I understand, honey. Look, I have an idea. What do you say to a compromise? Why don't you go to work tomorrow and spend the day working with the team and Brian? Then take a few days off, and the three of us can spend time doing whatever you and Claudia want to do. We can work on the wedding or just stay in, pop some popcorn and watch our favorite movies. You just name it."

She turned to Claudia. "What do you say, honey? Are you in?"

"Oh yes, I'm all in!"

Waving my index finger in the air with whatever strength I had left, I rolled my head on my neck. "Okay, that sounds fair, but if, and only if, something pressing comes up, I reserve the right to renege and go to the station."

Thumping her fingers on the table, Mom shook her head. "Okay, it's a deal!

Josh stood up at the table. "I think it's past time we take Allie and Claudia down to the apartment and get them tucked in. What do you say, Jake?"

"I couldn't agree more! I need some shut-eye as well."

Chapter 48

Promptly at seven o'clock the next morning, I walked into Brian's office. Looking through the observation window to the back room, he was setting up for work. When he looked up and saw me, he rushed out the door to me, opened his arms, and stopped short of grabbing me for a hug. "May I?"

Stepping forward, I opened my arms. "Of course!"

He wrapped his arms around me. "Allie, I am so glad to see you home safe and sound, but are you sure you want to come back to work so soon? You've been through so much in the past several months."

"Thank you, Brian, but I couldn't be surer. I wanted to be with you today to help with Payne."

"I know Payne would tell you to stay home, but I get it, Allie. I feel the same way. They offered to send the coroner up from York, but I refused."

Looping my arm through his, I exhaled. "Well, my friend, are you ready for this?"

"I'm not sure either of us could ever be ready for this, but it's what we need to do! I'm sure Payne would appreciate it. It would be in protest, but secretly he would be grateful."

As we stepped through the door to the back room of the morgue, I hesitated. "Has this room always been so cold, Brian?"

"Yes, this is the normal temperature. Why?"

"I don't know. It just feels abnormally cold."

Stepping up to the table, Brian peered up at me. "Are you sure about this?"

"Yes, I'm sure."

As he pulled the sheet down, exposing Payne's face, tears welled in my eyes. Resting my hand on Payne's forehead, a few tears leaked from my eyes and fell to the table. "Oh, my God, Payne. I'm so sorry! This was all my fault!"

"No, it wasn't!"

I knew that voice before I even lifted my gaze to respond. "What are you doing here?"

Raising his hands, he moved back and pleaded. "Please hear me out. Allie, I am filled with regret! I truthfully am! It was my fault! Everything was my fault!"

Brian moved to the door. "Allie? Allie, what's going on?"

Putting my arm up, I motioned to Brian. "Stay put. It's Makya!"

I thought I would explode! "Are you kidding me? Why should I hear you out? Just look at what you've done, and this is just the last horrible thing you did while you lived this life. Never mind, in all the other lives you've lived!"

"I know, and I'm so sorry, I truthfully am. I am truly in your debt! When you returned and killed me as Calian, in a split second, all my lives flashed before my eyes, and I felt all the pain and suffering I had caused for centuries. I have been given the opportunity to stay in this parallel time, paying my debts to others in this life and their future lives."

"I don't believe you. How could I ever trust anything you say?"

"Believe me, Allie, I understand that. I plan to prove it to you, no matter how long it takes."

As I opened my mouth to respond, he disappeared. "He's gone, Brian!"

"Thank goodness. What did he want?"

"That's yet to be seen. He was pleading for—"

"For your forgiveness?"

"That's the strange thing. No, not at all. I mean, he did apologize, but his intention was to take responsibility for all his past sins. I guess time will tell."

Then it struck me. "Brian, is Makya's body here?"

Without answering, he walked to one of the refrigerated doors and slid the body tray out. Pulling the sheet down, he exposed Makya's face.

Wringing out my hands, I fidgeted as a chill ran down my spine. "You're on your own for this one. I want nothing to do with it."

"I'm glad you feel that way because you couldn't be part of his exam. Mainly because you're the one who killed him."

Moving on, we began Payne's autopsy. Everything was going well until Brian removed his brain. I could tell by the look on his face that something was wrong. "Allie, look, he had a tumor. It's located close to the brain stem."

"Oh no, do you think he knew?"

"By the looks of it, I would say that he would have had to know. Wait here, I'm going to make a call. I'll be right back."

As I waited for Brian to return, I heard Grandfather's voice. "Little Bird, Payne's death was not your fault."

"Grandfather?"

He appeared in front of me. "It was his time, my dear. If he had not confronted Makya at that very moment, a bleed to his brain would have taken him. It was his last great deed. I can tell you for certain, if he wasn't there, things would have gone very badly for you. What you need to know and remember is that he is at peace now."

When Brian returned, he confirmed Payne knew he was sick. The rest of the autopsy went as suspected. The official cause of death was a gunshot to the carotid artery, causing severe blood loss.

Chapter 49

That same morning, Jake and Josh showed up at the station with Brick in tow. They walked to Payne's office and paused just outside the doorway.

Turning to Jake, Josh lifted his arm, motioning. "After you, my friend. After all, this is your office now."

Entering, Jake moved across the room. Payne's jacket was still hanging on the hook behind the desk. "I think I'm going to leave that there for a while. It just seems like it belongs there. I can't believe Payne is gone."

Jake pulled out Payne's chair and sat down. "Have a seat, Josh. I think I want you to stay while I begin sorting through some things. Just look at this pile of mail." With a puzzling look, Jake picked up a large manila envelope. "This can't be right. It has my name on it with this address. It's too soon for me to be getting mail here. I have to admit, I'm a bit curious about what it could be."

Josh leaned in. "Well, open it and find out."

Spotting a letter opener on the desk, Jake picked it up, slipped it into the envelope, and carefully slit it open. "It looks like some sort of document."

Sliding papers from the envelope, he dropped them as a look of shock swept across his face.

Josh leaned in again. "What?"

"It's a copy of Payne's frigging Last Will and Testament."

"What?"

Picking up the envelope, he looked at the return address. "It's from his lawyer! It's his Will!"

They both sat there, stunned, until Josh broke through the shock of it all. "You were the closest thing he had to family. I kind of get that. Maybe he just left you his watch or something."

Jake started rifling through the paperwork. "Shit, I don't think so. Why didn't he tell me? It looks like he left me everything, even the log cabin."

"Ah, maybe because he thought you would object?"

Jake looked up in utter amazement. "I would have! He surely has some family, somewhere!"

"Look, Jake, call his lawyer. Payne must have a good reason for leaving everything to you. You won't know unless you ask."

Chapter 50

The investigation team met at one o'clock that afternoon for one last conference regarding Makya's case. Brian and I grabbed lunch and walked into the war room at twelve-forty-five sharp. As we entered, everyone stood and applauded.

Josh took my hand and led me to the conference table, where there was a giant sheet cake. I was dumbstruck. "What is going on?"

"Well, it's a congratulations-on-the-job-and-job-well-done-we're-all-glad-to-see-you celebration!"

Jake quieted the room. "Please, could everyone please take a seat?"

As we sat down, he continued. "I don't want to drag this out. I just have a few comments and announcements to make. I know everyone here would love to go home. Especially those who have been away from their families for months and traveling to help in this investigation. I want you all to hear it from me first. We are officially closing this case that has affected so many people from California on the West

Coast to us here in Maine on the East Coast. I am also happy to report that the district attorney from South Carolina has ruled that Makya was killed in self-defense. Therefore, he will not be filing charges against Claudia and Allie."

Jake paused for a second to take a breath and keep his composure. "I know it isn't lost on any of us; what a tremendous loss we have suffered from Payne's passing. The wake for Payne will be the day after tomorrow, from six to eight. Services will be the next morning at nine a.m. Both will be held at Heald and Black Funeral Home.

"It's my distinct honor to tell you all that I have been offered the position of captain and lead detective here at this station. After much consideration, I decided that I would be honored to try on Payne's shoes for a while. So, with great humility, I have accepted."

Everyone in the room sprang from their seats and filled the room with excitement.

Jake raised his arms. "Wait! Wait, I'm almost finished. Thank you all again! Thank you so much for all your dedication and hard work. I would like to ask Josh, Allie, and Brian to remain after this last announcement. So, last but not least, let's eat cake, and then with the exceptions of Josh, Allie, and Brian, you are all dismissed."

An hour later, everyone had said their goodbyes and were on their way home. As Jake requested, Brian, Josh, and I stayed behind. Sitting at the conference table, we all polished off our second piece of cake as Jake addressed us.

"I know you are all wondering why I asked you to stay behind. Well, it is this. I don't want to take Brian's assistant away from him, but Allie, I think you need some time off."

"But, Jake—"

"No, Allie, this isn't a request. It's an order. You have a wedding coming up soon. Have you set a date?"

"Well, funny you should ask. Josh and I discussed it last night and decided we don't want to wait too long. If we can pull it together, we would like to get married in about a month."

Jake stood. "That's perfect. You can take two weeks of paid leave now to make plans. Work for a week and then take three more weeks off for the wedding and honeymoon."

"But, Jake—"

"Nope, it's settled. Then, when you get back from that honeymoon, be prepared. I will be putting you to work, and I won't be so generous with time off. Deal?"

I hesitated. "Ah…"

He asked again, this time more firmly. "Deal?"

It was clear. There was no use arguing. "Okay, deal."

Chapter 51

As it turned out, Jake was right. I needed some time off. If for nothing else, to plan and pull our wedding together. As luck would have it, Mom had secured the York Harbor Inn for our reception. We also got the bridal suite and a second room for two nights. Of course, Claudia and I would have the bridal suite and the guys would share the second room the night before the big day. After all, Josh couldn't come anywhere near me the morning of the wedding.

I don't know how we managed it all, but we got everything done, and now the day before the wedding, all we had to do was enjoy the fruits of our labor.

At Jake's insistence, we had the rehearsal dinner at the cabin. Dakota had it catered as a gift for Josh and me.

As we arrived, I gazed around. Everything was reminiscent of Dakota's famous New Year's Eve parties, only more magnificent. It was as if he plucked everything from a fairy tale and put it here just for Josh and me. An enormous ice statue carved into a bride and groom sat on a table next to a spectacular champagne fountain. Rows and rows of lights glittered overhead, lighting up every room.

I spotted Dakota across the expanse and raced into his arms. Then, pushing him back, I wiped the tears from my eyes. "This is so beautiful, Dakota! Just look at me. I'm the bride. I can't ugly cry at my own rehearsal dinner."

Gazing down at me, he smiled. "You could never cry an ugly cry, Allie. You are way too beautiful for that. Please, enjoy your evening. You certainly deserve it!"

Looking into his eyes, I saw something I had never noticed. There was a longing there. How did I not see this before? It made me uneasy to see him in that way. Not knowing how to respond, I simply smiled, took his hands in mine, and reached up to kiss him on his cheek. "Thank you so much for everything, Dakota. You have made this evening a dream come true!"

Sliding my hands from his grip, I stepped away, still feeling anxious about the expression on his face and the unspoken emotion behind it.

I moved over to the head table that was elegantly arranged for the wedding party. Of course, Jake and Claudia were our best men and matron of honor. Josh's sister, Pamela, and my brother, Mark's wife, Tammy, were our bridesmaids, and the ushers were Mark and Dakota. Last but not least, Mark's kids, Jason, age seven, and Emma, age five, were the ring bearer and flower girl.

A few minutes later, George picked up a microphone. "Excuse me, could I get everyone's attention?" The room went silent. "Dinner is ready and is about to be served. Please, find your seats."

Once everyone was seated, George exhaled and cleared his throat. "I would like to begin this meal with a toast to the bride and groom." Turning, he drew me up from my seat, pulled me close, and whispered in my ear, "This is not just from me, but also from your grandfather and papa."

Looking out across the room, he began. "I have been asked to escort this beautiful young woman down the aisle tomorrow and present her to the groom so they can begin their new lives together. It would be my honor and privilege to do that. As her grandfather would remind us, the church will be full to the rafters, not just with those here in body, but all the ancestors of the ages to celebrate this most incredible day. I feel truly blessed to share this momentous day with them. So please, raise your glasses to this beautiful couple."

The entire evening, we were swept up in the excitement and romance of every moment. At nine-thirty, Dakota approached the head table. "Well, everyone, we have a row of limos outside awaiting you all when you are ready to retire. As for me, I think I'm going to call it a night. So, until tomorrow, then." Reaching out, he shook Josh's hand and kissed me on the cheek.

Chapter 52

It was my wedding day! The big day had finally come. As usual, I woke up to the sensation of a rocking boat in a tumultuous storm on the ocean as Claudia stood over me, jumping up and down.

"Wake up, sleepyhead, we have things to do!"

Opening my eyes, I reached out, grabbing both of her ankles. "Okay, come on, I'm getting seasick!"

Bouncing down to sit next to me on the bed, Claudia was bubbling with enthusiasm. "We have a slew of things planned for the day! After all, as your matron of honor, it's my responsibility to make sure that you don't lift a finger all day, and that everything goes perfectly."

"I know, so what do you and Mom have planned?"

"That's for me to know...."

Pausing, she pointed in my direction, waiting for me to finish the sentence.

"...and for me to find out!"

Pulling a pillow from the bed, I placed it on my lap, and, trying not to laugh, I said sternly, "Okay, Claudia, enough of our childhood rituals."

I tossed the pillow at her as hard as possible, and the pillow fight ensued until I threw myself on the bed screaming, "Uncle! Uncle!"

"Hey, Al, that wasn't fair at all! You caught me off guard!"

A knock at the door interrupted us.

"Hello! It sounds like you are having entirely too much fun in there!

It was Mom. I got up and opened the door to find her standing there with room service. "I hope you're hungry. We have a busy day ahead of us!"

Claudia jumped from the bed. "Great, I'm starved!"

Laughing, I stood there in amazement as she took a plate and began piling food like she hadn't eaten in a month. "Claudia, how can you possibly be so hungry after that meal we had last night?"

"God, Allie, that was eleven hours ago. Are you kidding?"

Mom hugged me. "Well, this is it, honey! I just wanted to give you a few things before you get ready. I'm going to leave you girls to enjoy the day. Tammy and Pamila wanted me to tell you they will meet you both at the spa at nine-thirty."

She handed me two small boxes and an envelope. "Here you go."

When I opened the first box, I found the hand-embroidered handkerchief I had made for my wedding when I made Claudia's. The second was a jewelry box.

Mom's hands shook as she nervously looked up. "This is an heirloom from our side of the family. It's from our homeland."

I opened the box and lifted a Scottish diamond and gold thistle pendant.

Claudia stepped over. "Allie, that is beautiful!"

Reaching out, I took my mother in my arms. "It's perfect, it's just perfect. It will look amazing with my dress!"

"Okay, honey, now the envelope, and then I'm out of here. It's from Guile and me."

"Are you sure you don't want me to wait for Josh and Guile?"

"I'm sure. Besides, it kind of goes with the necklace."

Sliding out the paperwork, I carefully unfolded it. It was an all-expense paid two-week trip to Scotland. As I raised my eyes, I saw my mother's face was lit up.

"Mom, are you kidding?"

"No, honey, I'm not. I hope you don't mind. I know Jake offered you the cabin for your honeymoon, but Guile and I really wanted to do this for you. We figured at worse, you would have two honeymoons. The dates can be changed for a future trip if you choose to stay with your original plans."

"Are you kidding? This will be the best honeymoon ever. I don't think Josh has ever been to Scotland. Geez, I haven't been there since, what, I was seven years old? Thank you, thank you so much!"

After a long and amazing day of pampering, I found myself with George, waiting at the back of the church for the wedding march to begin. A tear ran from his eyes as he leaned down to whisper, "I hope Josh knows what a lucky man he is!"

Offering him my handkerchief, I kissed him on the cheek. "I think we're both lucky to have found each other."

Then, as the wedding march began, he pulled out his own handkerchief. "No, thank you, I came prepared."

Starting down the aisle, Josh was at the altar, gazing at me, beaming from ear to ear. As I got to the altar, Claudia smiled, taking my bouquet of roses and thistle. Turning to George, he lifted my veil, kissing me on the cheek. Nodding his head with great approval in his eyes, he placed my hand in Josh's.

As George stepped back to join my mother, the Chaplin said, "And who gives this woman, Allie Callahan, to this man, Josh Sullivan, in holy matrimony?"

Mom and George both looked up and, in unison, said, "We do!"

And with that, I lost myself in Josh's beautiful blue eyes for the entire ceremony. I think I was in a trance until I heard the words, "Then, with the power vested in me, I now pronounce you husband and wife! Josh, you can now kiss your bride!"

Everyone in the church sprang to their feet when the organ music began!

As Josh was kissing me, Jake said, "Hey, Josh, you can come up for air. We have a reception to get to!"

Taking my flowers from Claudia, Josh and I headed back down the aisle arm and arm when something caught my eye. Looking up to the balcony, I saw Payne standing there, smiling, as he placed a kiss on his hand and threw it out to me.

Made in the USA
Middletown, DE
06 September 2024

59878732R00156